FOLK
TALES
FROM THE
CANAL SIDE

FOLK TALES

TALES

FROM THE
CANAL SIDE

IAN DOUGLAS

ILLUSTRATIONS BY
GARY CORDINGLEY

The
History
Press

First published 2021

The History Press
97 St George's Place
Cheltenham
GL50 3QB
www.thehistorypress.co.uk

British Library Cataloguing in Publication Data.
A catalogue record for this book is available from the British Library.

ISBN 978 0 7509 9054 7

Typesetting and origination by Typo•glyphix
Printed and bound in Great Britain by TJ Books Limited, Padstow,
Cornwall.

CONTENTS

FOREWORD

Our waterways are an important part of our heritage. Today, they are loved by a new generation of boaters, but the traditions of the original boatmen and women live on in stories handed down through the generations. This book shares their tales in the time-honoured way of storytelling. In these folktales, Ian shares with us the toils and laughter, humour and hard work of the characters of the cut.

The Industrial Revolution was fuelled by the canal network and the boatmen and women were the life-blood of it. Today, our canals are no longer corridors of industry, they are an important leisure resource that is enjoyed by millions of people each year for its heritage and environment. Sadly, we no longer have many original boat families left but their lifestyles can be remembered through these folktales from the canal side.

Julie Sharman,
Chief Operating Officer, Canal & River Trust

A WORD TO OUR CANAL BOATMAN

Don't waste the Company's water by drawing the paddles before the gate is well shut.

Don't 'jam' a lock to spite your neighbour. It is like the dog in the manger, who would not eat the hay himself, nor would he let the horse eat it. Better give way and be happy.

Don't urge your horse unduly, in order to be first at the lock. Such a race does the Animal more harm in ten minutes than will a whole, but steady, day's work.

Don't swear at your horse, your Donkey, your Wife or Children when you are vexed. At such times it would be a good thing to pause and count fifty; a better thing to laugh and be merry; better of all to pray.

Don't work hard day and night and then take your earnings to the sign of the 'Pig and Whistle'. If you do, I fear the Publican will get the Pig, and you and your family will get the whistle, and a very sorry tune it will play.

Don't say you will never sign the pledge again because you have broken it once. Sign it again if you have broken it a score times. Like a drowning man, clutch at anything you think will save you, seek the help of God, and you will overcome the power of strong drink.

E. Clarke

ABOUT THE AUTHOR

Ian Douglas is a storyteller, who works extensively across the British Isles. With over twenty years of experience delivering storytelling, performance and theatre activities for schools, arts organisations, communities and festivals across Britain, he has developed a practice approach that mixes sensitivity, comedic energy and wit, leading to a style all of his own.

During his careers, Ian has worked as a theatre practitioner in residence for organisations across the North including Northern Stage and Live Theatre in Newcastle and, most recently, Theatre by the Lake in Keswick. Ian has had the privilege to sit at the knee of renowned storytellers such as Duncan Williamson, and at present is apprenticed to the First Laureate for Storytelling, Taffy Thomas.

The origins of Ian's work are steeped in the traditions of street theatre and this has helped him to develop his unique storytelling style. His work has been described as 'truly inspirational' and draws upon a rich vein of British folk tales and world myths.

Ian hails from West Yorkshire but now lives with his wife, Jo, on a narrowboat called *Hawker*, wherever the neighbours are nice.

What I love about storytelling is its simplicity. Stories meet us halfway and we, the audience, have to be complicit for them to be successful. The stories I like to tell are fun, inviting and light-hearted – even the serious ones! I believe that storytelling has a unique ability to connect people, not only to each other but to the past, the future and to the world around us.

Ian Douglas

ABOUT THE
ILLUSTRATOR

Gary Cordingley is a professional storyteller and illustrator living in Cornwall, where he is the south-west area representative for the Society for Storytelling. He is currently working hard at promoting storytelling events for adult audiences across south Cornwall. Having recently graduated from the authorial illustration MA at Falmouth University, Gary is busy developing the connections between oral and visual storytelling and is delighted to have been commissioned to illustrate this beautiful book by his long-standing friend and fellow storyteller, Ian Douglas. You can find more information about Gary's storytelling and illustration work on his website www.garycordingley.co.uk.

ACKNOWLEDGEMENTS

When I asked The History Press if they would be interested in me putting this book together and they said yes, I foolhardily thought it would be a hop, skip and a jump to assemble it. How wrong I was – so my thanks really need to go to them for their patience.

I need to extend my deepest gratitude to the Canal & River Trust staff at Ellesmere Port, who kindly took us in, gave us tea and their time and let us leave paper everywhere.

The kids also need a mention because they have put up with my huffs and puffs, so to Orin, Ellie, Holly and Amy – sorry, I will cheer up now. To Pete and Dave, for the stories you gave us, I hope the book does them justice. Thank you to Gordon and Jackie for the help and advice. To *Hawker*, our home, without which we wouldn't have had the inspiration.

Thanks must go to my friend Gary Cordingley who has brought the stories to life with his fine illustrations and of course to Katherine Soutar-Caddick for the cover image.

But mostly, thanks go to my wife, Jo. It's our book really – without her, it wouldn't have got done – and that's the truth, now and forever, lovely lady.

INTRODUCTION

When I was young, me and my mates used to play on the canal. I grew up in Huddersfield, in West Yorkshire, a town that owes a lot to its canal heritage. Sadly, when I was a kid, most of the Huddersfield narrow canal had been drained and people used it as a glorified bin.

Our favourite game was jumping the locks. We would take it in turns to run as hard as we could and then leap across from one side of the lock to the other, something I wouldn't even dare to attempt now. Luckily, none of us fell in – goodness knows what damage we would have done to ourselves if we had.

When we got bored with that little game we would, if we were feeling really brave, go and throw stones at the boats in the marina. Now, I know what you're thinking, but it was just the thing we did, as far as we were concerned, they were posh people who had boats. I wouldn't have liked to have had us lot around back then.

Thankfully, the canal in my home town is now fully operational and as you travel out of Standedge Tunnel and down the many locks, finally arriving in Aspley Basin, you can see the regeneration that it has, once more, brought to the areas it travels through.

And so, as I'm writing this, I'm struck by the irony of me now living on the canal. It is our home, and it has been for the last eight years. We live on narrowboat, *Hawker*. She is a 70ft-long Norseman and was built by a company called Hancock & Lane, who were, by all accounts, a well-respected boat-building company. *Hawker* is her third name, she was originally called *Honermead* and belonged to an estate that gave holidays to young people. The skipper's name was Captain Smith, an ex-Rolls-Royce engineer, who apparently ran a very tight and tidy ship – he would turn in his grave if he saw the boat now. She was sold on and renamed by a private owner who converted her to live on; he called her *Megfern*, after his two daughters and that's the name she had when we moved on board.

Jo and I set off in her for the first time on Christmas Eve 2013. It was a really windy day, I remember that. I also remember that we had our first ever argument about five minutes into that journey, but we soon got the hang of her and of each other and we haven't looked back since. We are continual cruisers, which means we are always on a journey and we have to move on every two weeks, sometimes sooner, depending on where we moor up – but that suits us down to the ground. She has to come out of the water about every three years to have her bottom blacked, it's a messy job but it's an important one, because if you don't do it you might go really rusty and eventually sink, which is not a good thing for a boat. The last time she was out, we took the opportunity to rename her. (Just so you know, it's considered bad luck to name a boat while she's in the water. I'm not a superstitious person but there's no point taking chances.) So, she is now *Hawker* and if you're ever passing, you are very welcome to come in for a brew.

People come to storytelling from all manner of directions. I grew up in a working-class household. When I was born my dad was a steel worker and my mum worked in the cotton mills as a doubler, but of course all that was gone by the time I left school. Thatcher and her lot put an end to that work, so I had to find something else.

I don't remember there being many books in the house but there were stories; uncles and aunties who told all manner of tales about the wider world. My grandad was from Liverpool and he told us he lived near Ken Dodd, the comedian. Apparently, he had my grandad to thank for his famous teeth – it was a fight over a bike and my grandad won.

And so, for a long time, I've collected stories without really considering why, just that they spoke to me in some way. However, lately I've had a feeling that it's time to dig a little deeper, to find those stories that might bring things closer to a full circle and so I've collected these.

The stories in this book are about real people, who did real things and lived real lives. I also think of them as 'my' people and as I've written the stories down I have put a face to each and every one of them – they are the faces from my life.

And so, here we are, you and I. I've been telling stories now for over twenty years but I've never written a book before so I hope that you will be kind. I also hope that you enjoy it; we've worked hard at it and all of the stories inside are true. The other thing they are is ours, the stories inside this book are as much a part of our heritage as they are the boaters' and I do hope that when you read them you will in some way feel a connection with them, as I do.

ABOUT GETTING STARTED

Something New is the Cry in this wonderful age
And Novelty charms both the Peasant and sage.
So to me, it appears that the task doth belong
To tug out from my brain box another new song.

The subject, I trow, is most near to us all
Nothing less than the flooding our growing Canal
Which with labour and years to perfection shall rise;
A giant was once but an infant in size.

(Traditional song)

Starting is always the hardest thing. Once you start the journey, it gets easier. It's a bit like pulling away from the bank, there's a push and at first there's nothing, no movement, and then she shifts and, slowly but surely, you're away …

And who knows where you will end up, so let's start, and where better than the place I'm sat right now. I'm sat in my chair in front of the fire on the Caldon Canal. The Caldon Canal runs from Etruria, in Stoke-on-Trent, to Froghall, in the pretty Churnet Valley, and boasts many fine sights along its 17 winding miles. One of the finest, and I know many would agree, is the Hollybush Inn at Denford – a good boaters' pub at that.

Well, most evenings, sat at stool near the bar you will find a man called Dave Rhead; he gave me this one.

THE DEVIL IN THE STOVE PIPE

Going back a long while from now there was an old woman called Mary. Mary lived on a boat no more than 40ft long and, the thing was, she also worked from it. Inside her back cabin she had a little wood-fired stove with a nice big hotplate on it and every morning around 6 o'clock she would stoke up that stove until it was nice and hot and she would make oatcakes, hundreds of them, and she would wrap them in paper to keep them warm and then sell them to the workers at the potteries of Stoke-on-Trent.

Well, Mary, she was good at the oatcakes. In fact, she was so good that she could hardly make enough of them and people would say, 'Mary, them oatcakes would tempt the Devil himself, they would', but you see, that put the fear into Mary because she was a godly woman and the thought of the Devil coming for her oatcakes was as worse a thought as there could be.

Anyway, Mary's biggest problem was that she was so busy with the oatcakes that she never had time for her boat – it was a right state and a half, I'll tell you. It was

the tattiest little boat on the cut and the inside was no
better. Worse than that, though, Mary wasn't looking
after herself. She hadn't much food in the cupboards,
her clothes were threadbare and worn, and with winter
coming there was nowhere near enough wood stacked to
keep the stove alight.

One winter's night, Mary was heading home from
a long day selling oatcakes and she could see along the
towpath a long line of boats moored in the darkness. The
lights of the boats reflected on the still water and smoke
was rising from stove pipes and it made her smile to see it,
but then she remembered that she had no kindling, the
small bits of dried wood sticks with which to easily light
her fire. She started to panic at the thought of a long night
in the cold.

As she made her way along in the dark she noticed
that the boat tied up behind hers had a stack of kindling
sitting on the back deck, minding its own business. Well,
she knew that it was wrong, but she thought to herself,
'Just a few sticks won't go amiss and desperate times lead
to desperate measures. I can just as easy replace them in
the morning.' She quietly stepped on to the deck and
borrowed an armful and quickly rushed home to light the
stove. Later that night she sat in the warmth of her fire
and chuckled lightly to herself.

Well, here is where I would like to impart a little bit of
friendly advice that will put you in good stead if you ever
find yourself living on the cut. You should never EVER
step onto someone else's boat without asking first – it's
just not the done thing. Knock on the side of the boat and
wait to be invited on first. And be aware that people who
live on boats can often tell by the smallest movement of

the water what is happening outside without needing to look, especially if a person was to step on board uninvited. Little did Mary realise it, but the man she stole from had felt his boat shift and so the next night he was waiting …

The following evening came, and once again Mary was heading back home after a long day's work. If the first night had been cold then this night was colder, and she had to pull her shawl tight around herself to keep warm. She suddenly remembered that once again she had no kindling to start the fire. One time could be called 'borrowing' but a second time is ungodly, and as she helped herself to a small amount of kindling from her neighbour's boat, she thought, 'Right, tomorrow I shall replace all I've taken and make my peace with God.'

What she didn't know was that this evening, the old boy inside was watching through a gap in the hatch. He saw everything, and he thought to himself, 'Right, two can play at that game!' In the last hours of the day he hatched a little plan.

Well, it just so happened that in a little tin at the back of a drawer in the boatman's cabin of the old boy's boat was a small amount of black powder – gun powder to you and me – anyway, the next morning as Mary was off up at the potteries making good trade, the old boatman, he took some of the kindling from the pile on his back deck and slowly, with the aid of a curved needle normally used to stitch boat canvas, he started to make small holes in the wood, just big enough that he could stuff them with the black powder. Finally, when he was happy with his work, he carefully made the pile up again on his back deck and sat satisfied, waiting for the plan to play out.

✿

Well, the third and final night of the story came around and, as we all know, three is the magic number in stories. Mary was making her way down the towpath in the dark, and as she came close to her neighbour's boat she stopped in the darkness, just to make sure there was no one around.

As quick and as quiet as she could, and knowing full well that she hadn't even attempted to fend for herself or replace what she had stolen, she nipped on to the back deck, picked up the wood and had it away home. Well, once could be deemed as borrowing and twice could be seen as ungodly, but three times – well, that is the work of Old Scratch, the Devil himself.

Once she was safely inside she opened the stove door and made a neat pile in the cold ash of the night before and put a spark to the wood. A little flame started to glow as the kindling caught so she shut the door and opened the vents to let the fire grow … and grow it certainly did. The black powder ignited and went off with such a blast that it blew the stove pipe right off the top of the boat.

But, you see, as the soot and the smoke settled, Mary was standing there with a blackened face, ash all around her and all she could think was that the people of the potteries had spoken the truth, it must be Old Scratch, the Devil himself coming down her stove pipe to steal her oatcakes. As quick as a flash, she packed up her boat and was never seen on the Caldon Canal again, leaving the old boatman to sit by his fire and chuckle.

We were boarded once. Late at night when me, Jo and the kids were fast asleep, someone got on the front of our boat. We were somewhere up on the Rochdale Canal and the area had a bit of a reputation, so we had moored up as close to a twenty-four-hour supermarket as we could, just to be on the safe side. In the middle of the night, I felt the boat move and I knew straight away that someone was on. As quick as a flash, I was up and running down the boat. I saw a face at the front-door window and then, whoever it was did a runner. Well, my adrenaline was up and so I gave chase up the car park. It was only when I got closer to the street lights that I remembered – I had no clothes on! Well, the sight of that would be enough to scare anyone away …

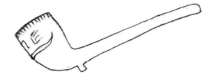

About the Navigators

Nightmares, Mother had, of navvies in the cellar
And dark eyes looking through the window outside
How we used to vex her and how we used to taunt her
How we would laugh and chant to her dismay
'Ware out Mother there's a navvy in the cellar
And two more looking through the window outside.
(Part of a traditional song printed in the
Journal of the Folk-Song Society, Vol. 8 [1930]).

It's really very easy as you move along the canal, whether that be by boat, bike or on foot, to get lost in the tranquillity of the place. I certainly do it as we travel along on *Hawker*. It doesn't matter if you are travelling through a rural or urban setting, be it the towering Pennines on either side of your view or the straight and angular buildings of a city centre, it's very easy to navigate your way without considering that none of this is natural. What I mean is, it wasn't there until we put it there. And it's only when you realise that, can you start to appreciate the enormity of the task that was the building of the canals.

But who did build the canals? If you put that question into your search engine it will bring up names like James Brindley and John Smeaton, the great engineers of the Industrial Revolution, and certainly the Duke of Bridgewater has his place. However, it's not the answer to the question – the real answer is, the navigators.

The navvies were gangs of itinerant manual labourers who literally 'cut' (an alternative name for the canal) the land to create our waterways. Their way of life was brutal, and death was an ever-present figure. Shifting up to 20 tonnes of earth and rock every day with nothing but a pick and a shovel, and living in temporary shanty towns, they moved across the country like an army, and wherever they went their reputation went with them – and the reputation they carried was bad. Strong drink, foul language and fighting were what settled folk knew of them, which was a story the newspapers of the time loved to print. But were these men as bad as the stories would have you think? Well, we found this old tale that shows an ever so slightly different side to these hardest of men. I do hope that you enjoy it.

The common misconception was that all navvies were Irish – it's not true. In fact, during the time of the construction of the canals, about 80 per cent of the navigators in England were English. They were largely made up of ex-farm labourers who had been forced to find new employment due to mechanisation. But the Irish did come, and they were happy to take lower wages for the same work, which eventually caused the undercurrent for this tale.

THE FIGHTING NAVVIES

It was around midnight, in a low-lit tavern just outside Sheffield, that two navvies met. They huddled around a table, neither of them alone for they both knew that witnesses would be needed to confirm the agreement settled by this conversation. These were no ordinary men, and the coming together of them had been long awaited within the navvy community.

The two men in question were Gypsy Jo and Bulldog Jack, both prized bare-knuckle fighters, and although they were there to set a date and time to fight, there was much more at stake. The men knew that the rising tension within their community between the English and Irish workers was about to spill over and who knew what trouble that would lead to. Both knew that if something wasn't done to settle the ill feeling, war would break out and war only leads to one conclusion, and so they met.

After what felt like an hour but, in reality, had only taken minutes, everyone present understood that the two men would meet and fight until one or the other submitted and hands were shook. They understood that wagers were allowed to swap hands and whatever money was taken was fairly won, but that this was not the real prize. Everyone present heard and understood and agreed that Jo and Jack would fight on behalf of their own, so that others wouldn't have to, and when the fight was done so too would there be an end to the hostilities.

And so they met, on a fine spring morning in March at the agreed place, Sheffield Basin, and the place was teeming with people. On one side of the water was Gypsy

Jo's camp, Jo couldn't be seen for the men that surrounded him, all talking loudly with advice. On the other side stood Bulldog Jack, who towered above the others around him, not talking – they knew well not to talk to him before a fight.

There were three ways into the basin and all ways were blocked by navvy men. This was not for outsiders, and those who tried to gain entrance were forcefully turned around and, of course, it wasn't too long before news of the event started to spread around the city.

The noise in the Basin that day was raucous, there was money to be made from the fight and there was not a man among them who could afford to pass up the opportunity to make in one day what it would take them a month in hard labour. But there was a strange tension felt by everyone present. Everyone knew that what was at stake here was more than money, but they had agreed to the terms of the fight.

Eventually there was movement. Jo appeared from among his crowd and it was easy to see as he made his way over a footbridge that he was ready for the task – a grim determination was set in his face.

The two men finally came nose to nose, eyes locked, and a ripple of excitement spread through the crowd. Two referees had been agreed upon, one from each camp, and a thick Belfast accent came out of one of them as he spoke the rules that both men had heard so many times before. They shook hands for the last time, put up their fists and the battle, so eagerly waited for, began.

The sounds of that meeting would stay in the memories of everybody in attendance for a very long time. Knuckle on chin, fist on flesh echoed across the Basin but it was evident from the off that there would be no quick finish to this fight. The two fighters were so equally matched that no one could see an end to it and, seeing this, the crowd's noise grew louder. All called sides, all shouted coarse words of encouragement, hoping that by being louder it would somehow turn the tide.

Suddenly, Gypsy Jo sent a clenched fist into the side of Bulldog Jack's head, which caught him off balance. The strike itself didn't hurt Jack that much, it was just another blow to suck up, but it did send him reeling into the crowd and as he fell, those behind fell too.

The problem was that as one of the bystanders struggled to remain on his feet, his arms flayed and his outstretched hand caught the side of the head of another, who thought that the knock was intentional. Not knowing where it had come from, he hit the nearest unknown person, who in turn hit back and now there were two fights happening side by side. Well, someone tried to stop the sideshow but this only led to others getting involved and before anyone knew it the fight had spread throughout the crowd. More and more men raised their fists, tempers spilt over, the terms of the fight were off – war broke out.

Meanwhile, in the city of Sheffield, news of the riot had spread and with it so did the worry. If the fight was to spill out into the streets, all manner of damage could be done to both property and life. People eventually grew so concerned that they went to implore the Peelers to take action, but the Peelers were in no way stupid, they knew their limitations, the navvies had no love for lawmen and any Peeler foolish enough to try to even enter the Basin that day would have the entire group of fighting men to contend with and that was not something that any of them were brave enough to do.

There was only one way to deal with this situation, said the Peelers, and that was to turn to God. Only a priest could help them now. The only person the navvies would fear more than their own mothers would be the priest and so word was sent to the man who had the unfortunate luck of being the priest of that parish and he was Father Anderton.

At the time of this story, Anderton was in his dotage. His voice was as weak as his back and, if the truth be told, his faith was stretched somewhat, so when they came to his door to plead with him to try and stop the fight before it was too late and the city was ransacked, Father Anderton replied that he didn't really see what good he could do. He did, however, agree to attend.

Father Anderton made his way on frail legs to Sheffield Basin, by which time the battle was really settling in. The scene that he witnessed could have been likened to a slaughter house; blood and bodies lay everywhere, and it turned his stomach. He was, however, committed and so he decided to find high ground. He made his way to the footbridge steps and once he was high enough that he could see above the crowd, Father Anderton started to speak the words of God.

Well, the story doesn't say what words Father Anderton spoke that day but even though they were quiet, frail words, to his amazement among the crowd of fighting men some stopped to listen. Individuals, blood streaming from cuts and broken noses, wiped away the grime of the fight and stood open-mouthed, listening to the priest – and it spread.

Father Anderton couldn't believe it and as he saw the effect that his words were having on the men, his diminished faith started to grow. Maybe, he thought to himself, maybe the power of the Lord truly was inside him. His voice grew in weight and power until all present stopped their evil pastime and listened. He watched as the words hit home like blows from the Almighty. Grown men hung their head and flinched; some openly cried, but Anderton wasn't done. Suddenly he believed in his heart that he could change these men for the better and so he raised his voice again, and as he did, he closed his eyes allowing the words to flow from his heart.

But then Father Anderton had the strangest feeling, as he felt the power of the Lord take over him, using him as a conduit through which to bring these sinners back into the flock. He suddenly had a sensation of being lifted from the ground, high above the heads of the gathered men, and as he was lifted he had a fleeting sensation of being one with God himself, like he had spread the wings of angels and was now flying above his flock.

It was then that Anderton opened his eyes – only to realise that this was far from the truth. As he opened his eyes he realised that it wasn't God who had elevated him at all, it was Gypsy Jo and Bulldog Jack. The two men had lifted him as gently as a mother would lift their child and carried him across the Basin and up through the streets of Sheffield. Onlookers with open mouths witnessed them take him all the way to the Grosvenor Hotel, in through the swing doors, and place him gently on a stool. They bought him a drink, patted him on the back and silently returned to their friends, where they promptly continued the fight.

The story doesn't tell who won out that day, but I like to think that they fought with a smile on their faces.

When I left school at 16 and I wandered wide-eyed into the world of work, one of the jobs I took on for a very short time was as a barman in the Royal Unicorn pub in Huddersfield. It could get wild in there at times and there were all manner of people frequenting the place, but I was asked one day, by a mountain of a man with hands like shovels, if I owned a pair of stout boots, to which I replied, 'Yes'.

He told me that if I wanted some hard but well-paid work, I should be stood in them boots at 5.30 the next morning on the side of Leeds Road where a van would pick me up and I would get good employment – and if I worked hard I might be asked back again. When I asked the man what work it was, he looked at me, downed his drink in one gulp and then with a grin, simply said, 'You're off to work with the navvies …'

I've still got them boots somewhere. It's true!

We were really privileged to be asked to tell stories at Sheffield Basin to help celebrate its 200-year history just two years ago. We worked with our friends from Impossible Theatre and Tom Wright from the Canal & River Trust, to breathe life into some of the old stories and canal history. It was a great event and wonderful to see so many people in attendance – great after party, as well, but that's another story.

About the Working Boats

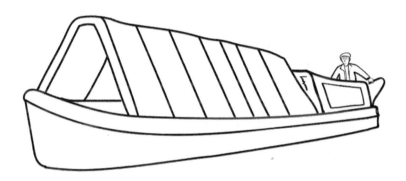

There are a number of things that, as you chug along the cut, make your heart beat just a little bit quicker. The flash of a kingfisher; the moment that the landscape opens up as you pass over an aqueduct; the sight of your wife bringing you a hot brew when you have been stood out in the cold for hours in the rain while she sits by the fire, 'making sure it's not going out,'; and of course, the sight of an old working boat moving through the water.

They move differently to modern boats – lower in the water, more purpose – and the sight of them reminds you of a different time to ours. The time of the Industrial Revolution was the golden age for working boats and carrying companies sprang up right across England, shifting goods to feed the growth of our expanding towns and cities. At this time, the country's road systems were poor, to say the least, and pack horses were really the only way to transport wares from place to place, but as the age of the narrowboat dawned so did our country's advancement as an industrial leader in the world, such was the impact of the working boat.

The Grand Union Carrying Company Ltd and Fellows, Morton & Clayton Ltd were by far the biggest of the many companies working the cut, but this story concerns a Number One. I love to catch sight of a Number One because when I see one, I know I'm not looking at a company, I'm looking at a boat owned by an individual or a family who ran their own fortunes – they really lived the life of the cut. What follows is a story about one such boat that had unfortunately fallen on hard times.

THE CLINK OF THE STEERING CHAINS

Well, there was once two brothers who came from somewhere up near Hull and so alike were they that people said they were like peas in a pod. They did everything together – they lived together, they played together, they fought together and eventually they worked together, and they ran a boat, a Number One, and they ran it as well as they could.

At first, all was well and for many years they did good trade hauling goods up and down the River Trent but, over time, work became scarce and times had turned hard, what with the coming of the railway. The boys found themselves getting poorer and poorer.

So, they were mighty pleased when one early evening they were asked to take a load full of good timber from Hull to Lincoln with a promise that if they made good time there would be a return load, which would double their profits. This was the very news that the brothers needed and they slept lightly in their beds that night thinking about the day ahead.

The job started well, it was a fine crisp autumnal sunrise, and the sky was looking clear; a perfect day for boating. The boys pulled the boat into Hull dock for loading and the timber was craned aboard. The boat's body settled down into the water under its weight and as they watched the boys could see the quality of it and knew that they would get a good price for hauling the load. Eventually, after what felt like an age, the brothers received the nod to say that they could get the journey under way.

Some days are made for a journey and this was one of them. There wasn't a wisp of wind in the air to fight against and every lock seemed to be set ready for them. They made good progress as they weaved their way through the landscape. In fact, things were going just a little too well when they came up on the Fossdyke Navigation, a stretch of water that is, even to this day, notoriously shallow – and that's where things started to go wrong.

The first thing the brothers noticed was that the boat seemed to be making little headway. The engine was working almost flat out but they seemed to be just edging forward and at times at a standstill. They struggled on like this for what felt like an hour, pushing the engine harder and harder before they heard and felt the boat touch the bottom and she ground to a complete standstill.

Well, the engine was put into idle as the boys turned to the barge poles, using the long lengths of wood to try and push the boat out into deeper water, but there just wasn't any, and so, after some time, they gave up and one of the boys walked the distance to Lincoln to get help. Their only alternative was to offload half of their precious cargo and take a cut in their earnings.

Eventually, they offloaded what was left of the timber at Newsum Wharf. Once it was weighed in and they had paid the toll fee, the boat was reloaded with a variety of thankfully much lighter goods and with a gloomy mood about them they set off back to Hull. However, by this time it was near sunset, so they made plans to push on in the dwindling light, past the dreaded Fossdyke, to take the opportunity to moor up for the night in Knaith Park at Torksey.

As they reached their stop for the night, the brothers were in a foul mood. They pulled the boat in close to the bank and they worked silently to drive mooring pins into the soft bank. The ropes were tied firmly and, satisfied that the boat was safe, they went into the back cabin to huddle round the stove. They had been hoping that after a hard day's work they would be resting in a local ale house, a hearty meal on the table and jugs of porter to wash it down, but no such luck.

It was now dark outside and under the dim light of the cabin's lamps the brothers began to discuss ways to bulk out their profits. They knew Knaith Park well and had chosen the stop for more than one reason – rabbits. Rabbits brought a fair price, if you knew where to sell them, and there were enough inns and hotels in Kingston upon Hull that were happy to take them without asking too many questions. It was a risky idea because the game-keepers were keen in that area and carried guns, but the boys knew their business and, as they say, 'Desperate times lead to desperate measures', and so with snares in hand the brothers set off into the dark.

They worked quickly and quietly, moving across the field setting snares wherever they found rabbit trails, and after a couple of hours they had covered a fair patch of land. So, it was time to turn back to the start and hope that they had a catch – and that's when it all went wrong.

As they turned to make their way back, they found themselves blinded by a gamekeeper's light and the man shouted for them to stay still and that he had a gun. The two boys stayed as still as stone as the keeper approached them, his light in their faces and gun pointing straight, but he hadn't reckoned on how close these boys were – 'like peas in a pod'.

So close were they that there were no words needed and they attacked as one. They quickly overpowered the gamekeeper and knocked him to the ground, but as he fell the man brought the gun round and had one of the boys in its sights. However, his brother was quicker, and he managed to grab the barrel as the trigger was pulled. A loud bang rang out over the fields, but the brother pulled the gun free of the keeper's grasp and swung with all his might, bringing the butt down on the man's head. They heard the crack and the keeper lay dead, blood leaking from the wound.

They crouched there in the darkness. The only sound was their laboured breath as they waited to see if the shot would bring others, but nothing, no sight or sound, and so together and without discussion they dragged the lifeless man over the rough ground back to the boat. They knew that they had to hide him and so they took him to the aft of the boat and slowly wrapped the boat's steering chains around his body and then lowered him into the water, manoeuvred him under the boat and secured him against the hull.

That night, the brothers lay awake in their bunks, with the flames of the stove flickering across the cabin's walls. Both had their eyes wide open, but neither spoke – neither dared. But the place wasn't silent.

As they lay, unable to sleep, all they could hear was the scraping and rattling of the steering chains hitting the metal hull of the boat. It wouldn't stop, and they couldn't escape it even when they buried their heads in the blankets. It was a very, very long night.

As dawn came, the brothers were near scared to death. They could hardly look at each other and their conversation was hushed and quick. Like two people in a trance, they cast off and made a very hurried journey to Hull. When they arrived at the dock, no one could get a word out of them. They walked side by side quickly through the streets until they reached the police station and only then did they tell their story.

The boys were put under lock and key as the police went to investigate the crime and, a number of hours later, they were brought into a room to be charged. They sat at a table with their heads held low, only to be told that as thorough as the search had been, no body or any evidence of a body could be found and if there was no body then there was no crime.

The brothers were released that day and were free to continue with their lives, but how could they go back to their boat? And so they sold it and never went near the cut again. There is no happy ending – how could there be?– to this tragic tale. The boys, 'like peas in a pod', could never escape the clinking of the chains, and slowly it drove them both mad and that is how they were to the end of their days.

⚭

For the last five years, Jo and I have taken *Hawker* down to the Etruria Boat Festival, at Stoke-on-Trent. It's a really lovely boat gathering that brings together old working boats for people to look at and learn about and is wrapped around with an arts and music festival run by our friends at B-arts. It lasts a weekend and is a highlight of our year.

It's a real pleasure to see so many old boats in one place and you can easily use your imagination to take you back to a time when all you would see on the cut were narrowboats shifting goods like coal and flour, clay to the potteries, and all manner of things across the country. *Hawker* stands out a little bit among all the old working boats but then we open our home up and people can come aboard for a brew and a story about times gone by, so I think we play our part.

ABOUT THE TUNNELS

Approaching the entrance to a tunnel is always a special moment for me; each one is different – different length, different head room and, I think, different feel.

The shorter tunnels are unmanned and, other than switching your headlamp and navigation lights on, there's not much else to do than get on with it, but the long ones take a bit of preparation.

You stop and moor up; make sure your fire's not lit; open all your curtains and put all your lights on; get your big coat on, even in summer, then wait to be checked. The tunnel masters check your height, especially if you use your roof for storage, like we do. Anything they think will hit the roof has to come off and be stored elsewhere, and if you're still too high you fill up your water tank to take on extra weight. Then they check your lights and horn are working. If that's all good, you just have to wait your turn. If there's something not working, then there's a mad panic to find a hammer to hit it with. In some tunnels, a pilot comes with you because the tunnel has some obstructions to watch out for, so they need to talk you through.

Suddenly you get a signal and then you're off – on with the throttle, line her up and you're in. Once you're in there, you suddenly get a real sense of how determined human kind was that nothing would get in the way of progress. When you notice the intricate brick work that can, in some cases, go on for miles, you really feel the power of our hand. It might sound daft, but they actually built tunnels because it was cheaper to go through the hill than go to the trouble of going over it, which is slightly ironic when you consider that the famous Standedge Tunnel at Marsden took seventeen years to build and cost the lives of around fifty men. At just over 3 miles, it is the longest and deepest in the country.

But what really gets me when I'm in a tunnel is that it was all done by hand, no drilling machines and laser plumb lines, just picks, shovels and wheelbarrows. They built them without towpaths inside, so in the days before steam when boats were horse drawn, you would have to send the horse over the hill and 'leg' it through – a process by which a number of men would lay on balanced planks or the roof of the boat, put their feet on the tunnel roof and walk the boat through, often with the expense of paying a local 'legger', who was ever present around the tunnel entrances. We like to turn our engine off sometimes in shorter tunnels and get our children to leg *Hawker* through to the other side, just for the fun of it, but we just pay them in crisps and experience.

THE HARECASTLE TUNNEL

For more than 200 years, sightings of a headless ghost have been reported haunting the area around the famous Harecastle Tunnel in Staffordshire. The tunnel is on the Trent & Mersey Canal and connects the town of Kidsgrove with Tunstall in Stoke-on-Trent. It is 1.5 miles long and was originally built for the transportation of coal to the bottle kilns in the Staffordshire potteries.

Workers and boat people alike have always been wary of venturing out on days when the ghost has made an appearance, as it is thought to portend doom and disaster and has supposedly been seen on the morning of many a North Staffordshire mining disaster.

The question is, where did the ghost come from? Well, if you travel down the canal on foot, you will eventually arrive in the town of Stone. If you keep your eye out, you will come across a plaque mounted on the side of the towpath. And what's written there appears to be the most widely accepted story.

The plaque tells the story of the murder of Christina Collins, a young woman who, in June 1839, paid 1 shilling and sixpence to take a Pickford's boat from Preston Brook to travel to London to meet her husband. But she never made it.

What was a young woman doing travelling to London on a working boat? You see, as well as carrying goods, a lot of the working boats on the canals would agree to carry a limited number of passengers to make extra income. Passengers had to consider, when travelling by narrowboat, that this type of transport was a good deal slower than travelling by coach. However, this made it much cheaper and so was attractive as long as you weren't in a hurry.

So, the boat travelled south, through Harecastle Tunnel, and stopped for the night near Stoke-on-Trent. The next day, they continued their journey but it wasn't long after leaving Stoke that the three men in charge started to drink heavily. The air was blue with the language that they were using and most of that was in Christina's direction. So much so, that by the time they arrived in the town of Stone, Christina was worried enough to report her fears to the toll house. She did, however, receive little sympathy and was simply told to report the men at the end of her journey to London.

The next day, Christina was found in the canal near Rugeley, and the evidence of what had happened to her at the hands of the boatmen isn't for the likes of this book. The men didn't go unpunished, though. Two were hanged and the other deported. To this day, there is a wooden statue beside workhouse bridge, called 'Christina', in her memory.

However, we did a little digging around because there were a few things that just didn't make sense, especially the fact that the boat was well beyond Harecastle Tunnel when the terrible deed was done. Eventually we found two more possible origins for the boggart …

Dancing Lights

Samuel Wood was the kind of man who only believed what his eyes told him. He had no truck with stories of ghosts and spirits and would go out of his way to argue the toss against things like religion and such like. As time went on, Samuel Wood started to enjoy the many mild confrontations that he always seemed to find himself embroiled in as he sat of an evening at the bar of the many public houses along the towpath.

Samuel Wood was a boat owner and ran mainly coal on his 60ft narrowboat along the Trent & Mersey Canal. He ran the boat alone, for the main part, and so had plenty of time as he chugged through the countryside to form his thoughts about the world around him and, once formed, Samuel Wood's thoughts could not and would not be budged.

In the December of 1879, Samuel Wood moored his boat just outside Kidsgrove, in Cheshire. His plan was to moor up for the evening and then make his way further north the following day. The days being shorter, it was still early evening when the sun set and so he decided to take a walk down to a local public house that he hadn't had the chance to visit for some time, and as he set off down the towpath he was in high spirits – things were going well for Samuel Wood and his pocket was jingling with coins.

Before he even got the through the door of the pub, he could tell by the noise that there was a healthy crowd inside and after a number of days alone Samuel Wood was craving the banter. So, he pushed his way through the throng and managed to get to the bar and order himself a drink, found himself a spare stool, made camp and then turned his attention to the many conversations around him.

Well, this was a canal-side tavern and most of the faces around Samuel Wood were familiar, even though he couldn't put names to all of them. He wasn't a shy man and, being among his own, he soon found himself drawn into a number of different, fairly jovial bits of local gossip. However, one particular bit of conflab caught his attention.

Strange happenings had been reported near and around the towpaths leading to and from the Harecastle Tunnel. Unexplainable apparitions had been witnessed, accompanied by unearthly sounds that had tested the nerves of many a strong-willed man. Some said that it was a haunting, some said it was potent of doom; one man even went so far as to say that even the pitmen, whose stout hearts took them underground into the dark pit every day, refused to dig on the days a sighting had been reported through fear that it might bring the roof down upon their heads.

Samuel Wood listened in near disbelief as these grown men talked like scared children, telling fairy tales to each other until he could no longer bear it. He gave an angry shout that brought a moment of silence to the place and all heads turned in his direction. The silence lasted long enough to grow uncomfortable until the landlord broke it by asking Samuel Wood what he had to say about these things.

Well, after almost a lifetime of making his opinions known about things that go bump in the night, his script was well rehearsed, and Samuel Wood now had centre stage. So he set to, explaining at great length why everything he had heard was complete and utter rubbish. Every man present that evening listened until eventually Samuel Wood had finished his speech and silence once again descended, but this time no one broke it. Everyone just stood staring at Samuel Wood until he felt so bad for speaking out that he gave his good night and made to leave. He had just made it to the door when the landlord spoke once more; this time it wasn't a question, this time it was a challenge.

As Samuel Wood laid in his bunk the next morning, he realised that he was experiencing a sensation that he had never felt before and that, dear friend, was doubt. He had never doubted in his life that what he believed wasn't the absolute truth. There was no such thing as ghosts and goblins and if a thing couldn't be seen or held in your hand, then it didn't exist, but here he was watching the light of the day getting brighter, pulling his blankets around him and feeling a niggle of doubt about what he had agreed to do.

The challenge he had accepted was really very simple. He had agreed to take his boat, at midnight, to the entrance of Harecastle Tunnel and then, without the aid of his engine, leg his boat through to the other side. If he made it and nothing was seen or heard then there would be a public apology from the landlord on behalf of all present and all the ale he could drink, but if anything happened in the tunnel, or there about, that could not be explained, Samuel Wood, the doubter himself, would no longer talk ill of anyone's beliefs.

Samuel Wood busied himself that day with all manner of tasks that didn't need to be done, anything to distract him from that little bit of doubt niggling away at the back of his mind, until eventually the time came. With a last look at his pocket watch, Samuel Wood untied his boat and set off toward the mouth of Harecastle Tunnel. There was a lock to be navigated to get him to the entrance of the tunnel and as he opened the sluice gate to let the lock fill, Samuel was met by the landlord and a group of men who had come to make sure he set off on his journey. They wished him well and assured him that they would take the journey over the hill and meet him on the other side – and with that said, Samuel Wood set off to meet his fate.

He slowly chugged the short journey to the tunnel entrance, pulled the tiller hard right to line up the boat to enter Harecastle and then shut off the engine. The silence was deafening. Samuel Wood climbed onto the roof of his cabin, lay down on his back and waited to be submerged by the darkness. After what felt like an age, the boat was finally underground and Samuel Wood could put his mind to the simple task of legging his boat through the water. He lifted his legs and found the stone surface above him and started to push the boat forwards and, once he got momentum, the job wasn't that hard at all, his boat was unladen, so light enough in the water.

In fact, Samuel Wood actually started to feel good about the task. It was the first time he had felt happy all day, and as he pushed on through the dark his mind wandered back to the conversation the night before. 'Ghosts and ghouls,' he thought to himself. 'What a load of rubbish! There's nothing but this tunnel, this boat and the darkness. Is there not?'

Harecastle Tunnel is 1.5 miles long and after an hour Samuel Wood had just made it past the middle – the lowest section, in fact. It was so low that he had to move off the cabin roof, for fear of getting trapped, and let the boat move on her own. But, as he stood there on the back deck surrounded by pitch black, he became aware of a noise all around him. At first, he thought it must be a shaft of wind running through the tunnel but as he listened more intently, Samuel Wood imagined that it sounded much more like music. How could that be? But he was sure of it – there, in the very heart of the tunnel was music and, what's more, it was beautiful and growing in intensity, all around him and everywhere.

Samuel Wood was lost in a swirling world of sound, and he felt like he was perched on the edge of a cliff, unable to tell if it was elation or fear that he felt when suddenly, as abruptly as it had started, the music stopped, and with it his mood. He was plunged into a sadness he had never felt before nor ever would again.

And then, just as he thought all had returned to normal, he became aware that off in the distance there was light, could this be the light at the end of the tunnel? As quick as he could, Samuel Wood climbed back on the cabin roof and started to leg the boat again, this time with all his strength. He desperately wanted to reach the outer world and would happily tell others that he had been wrong all these years.

As he legged, he twisted his head to see if the light had grown larger, but when he looked his heart sank, there was now no light at all! It was only due to knowing which way the boat was pointing that Samuel Wood had any sense of direction, but what he didn't know was how far through the tunnel he had travelled. He felt desperate, and once again climbed down from the cabin roof to stand alone in the dark.

Samuel Wood cried out for help, but none came. He did, however, look behind him and there, to his horror, was the light again. But this time it was moving, and moving towards him, slow at first but gathering speed, and with it came the music, ever louder. The light and the sound hit him and slammed him into the back cabin door, taking the wind out of his lungs and pushing the boat forward faster than it had at any time that night.

With a struggle, Samuel Wood stood up and looked forwards, only to see the light hover toward the front of his boat and he saw how beautiful that light was. But it was also the last thing he saw or thought. The light shot forwards, and the music, too, and knocked him backwards. His head hit the tiller and Samuel Wood plunged into the cold, inky black water and never spoke again.

They waited at the mouth tunnel for what felt like an age for Samuel Wood's boat to appear – and appear it did, as did his body many hours afterwards, and he was buried in a local churchyard some days later. Not many attended, and how the story was pieced together I'm not sure, but that's how I heard it.

And as for the lights of Harecastle Tunnel, well, they have been seen many times since. But now, when they are, people don't work, they stay at home or huddle around tap-room fires and remember the fate of Samuel Wood.

A Perfect Match

Jim and Elsie should never have married, that was the general consensus among the friends and family of this feuding pair. Separately, they were a pleasure to be around and not a bad word would be spoken about them, but together … well, that was a very different story.

Their problem, as others saw it, was that neither of them was ever wrong and both had to have the last word. If Jim said, 'black', Elsie said, 'white'; if Elsie said, 'up', Jim said, 'down'. If Jim said, 'today', then Elsie would make sure that it was tomorrow, and on and on it went.

But that wasn't actually the real problem. The real problem was that they had both married the wrong person. Jim, well, he just wanted a simple life, a quiet life, a go to work, come home, put your feet up by the fire kind of life and needed a wife who was happy to provide. Whereas Elsie – Elsie was a showgirl on the inside and in her late teens had caught the eye of a travelling showman and was all but ready to do a flit when her parents caught wind of the plan, had the showman run out of town and carefully steered her towards Jim.

And so they bickered, day in day out, which at first was fine because Jim worked the boats and spent long days carrying salt from Middlewich to cities like Stoke-on-Trent and Birmingham and such like, whereas Elsie made home and tried her very best to be the little wife. But it didn't suit her, and both of them secretly hoped that the other would get so sick of the fight that they would up and leave. Of course neither of them would be the one to do it because that would put them in the wrong, you see.

Over time, Jim's work started to dwindle, what with the coming of the railway and the improvements made to the road networks. The boats were too slow to feed the growing needs of the expanding towns and cities of the North and so it wasn't too long before the pair were faced with a real dilemma, either Jim could quit the boat and find more profitable work or, and it was a very big or, the couple could give up the house and Elsie would join Jim on the boat, where they could live and work in harmony.

Late one night, Jim and Elsie sat in silence by the glow of a dying fire until eventually Jim spoke. He looked Elsie in the eyes and told her that he had thought long and hard and was sure that the right thing was to give it a go. He said that he knew he wasn't the man she needed but that marriage was marriage and meant hard graft sometimes, and you never know, he said to her, it might just work out.

Well, I would like to have been the one to tell you good news, but I can't. I would love to have been able to tell you that Jim and Elsie's decision to be together on that working boat, with its tiny little boatman's cabin, brought them together and it was just what they needed to stop their arguing and live a happy, loving life together and float off down the cut into a glorious sunset. I can't, I'm afraid, it's not that type of story.

Once on board, Jim and Elsie's lives went from bad to worse. Their inability to get away from each other meant that every little niggle one had about the other was magnified tenfold, and what was worse, they now started to interfere in each other's worlds.

Elsie went through the painful task of trying to make a boatman's cabin into a home, which of course meant that everything had to be shifted around and Jim couldn't find anything he needed. Everything had its place, and nothing was in its place, so every time Elsie's back was turned Jim moved things and Elsie hit the roof.

Jim had to go through the slow and painful task of trying to teach his wife how to run a working boat – how to tie up at night time, run locks fast, keep haulage logs and so on. Well, she was a fast learner, no doubt, but the problem was that Elsie always knew a better way of doing things and very often she was right, although Jim didn't like it and wouldn't admit it.

But the one thing that Jim had that he refused to share with his wife was the tiller. He would not, under any circumstances, let Elsie take control of the boat – and that was a real problem. Elsie saw it as an insult. How dare this man tell her what to do in her own home? And, to Jim, that was an insult. How dare that woman call his boat her home?

So, once again, they were at loggerheads.

Well, this tragic tale is swiftly coming to its conclusion because something had to give, and it happened like this, or so the story says. The pair were asked to make the journey through Harecastle Tunnel to take a load to

Stoke. It was morning when they set off and the weather was good, so this should have been a fairly easy job, but as they approached the tunnel and moored up to be inspected by the tunnel master before making passage through, Elsie decided that this would be the perfect time to be allowed to take control of the tiller; her reasoning being that underground there would be very little to do other than go straight with no fear of crashing just straight through to the other side.

Jim said, 'No, the tunnel is dangerous and no place for a woman to take control.'

Well, that was a red rag to a bull and drew the attention of the tunnel master, who was finding the whole thing very amusing. Elsie used his presence to her advantage and said, loud enough for everyone near to hear, that Jim wasn't man enough to let his wife take control and that only a real man could see it within themselves to support and encourage their wives to grow.

Jim stood for just a while in silence and then, red-faced, he simply went inside the cabin and closed the door, leaving Elsie to wallow in that glorious moment. She had won and for the first time ever her husband had backed down. Elsie took the tiller, the tunnel master waved her off and watched as she disappeared into the darkness with a very triumphant smile upon her face.

Over an hour later, the boat emerged through to the other side of the tunnel and if you had been there that day you would have seen a very contented look upon the skipper's face at the tiller as the boat glided out into the sunshine. But it wasn't a look of contentment on Elsie's face because she was nowhere to be seen. Jim stood proud, tiller in hand, and continued down the cut and the story doesn't tell what fate finally befell him. As for Elsie, she was never seen again. She never came out of Harecastle Tunnel, but they do say that her spirit has dwelt there ever since.

I'll sing you a song of the Junction Cut
I'm wedding you over the mopstick
Whether you like it or whether or not
I'm wedding you over the mopstick

[Chorus:]
Boaty, boaty, spit in the cut
Spit in the cut, spit in the cut
Boaty, boaty spit in the cut
I'm wedding you over the mopstick

(Traditional song)

❦

My wife Jo hates going through Harecastle Tunnel. She says that the sound and the lack of light disorientates her. This hatred of the tunnel obviously has an impact on her speed as she travels through because she can make a journey that is supposed to take about forty-five minutes last only thirty! Poor *Hawker*.

Our first experience of Harecastle didn't go quite as planned. Before we travelled through, we were met by the tunnel master, who was a great storyteller in his own right. He told us about the many stories to be found inside, but also said we should be careful because there were also modern tragedies. Only the year before, a man had lost his life when he hit his head on the low stone roof and drowned in the water.

We went through at a real crawl as he had told us to go through at our own pace, but when we emerged safely from the other side we were confronted by a very angry tunnel master, who told us, in choice words, that we had been in there so long he was about to come and drag us out … there really is no pleasing people!

ABOUT THE BRIDGES

Trudging along a well-worn track
Trailing a barge and pole
Off to the end of the world and back
Never a rest at the goal
Up to the hills and down to the sea
Who's for a trip with a sleepy barge?

(Traditional song)

I can't count the number of times we have been moving along the cut and been out in the middle of nowhere, with

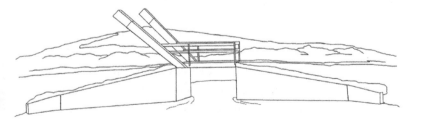

nothing but fields on either side and no grand houses or great estates to be seen. But then you come upon a bridge and there's no road across it. All it seems to do is to link one muddy field with another very muddy and unused field, but the bridge itself is beautifully constructed, an architectural triumph, and as you travel through it, you can't help but see the craftsmanship involved in its construction and you have to ask yourself, 'Why?'

Well it was Jo who looked into it and it turns out that there's more to those bridges than meets the eye. You see, unlike tunnels, bridges were not built to make it easier or cheaper for the engineers and they weren't built to save the navvies a mound of extra backbreaking work, no, they were built because of an Act of Parliament that was created to ensure that no one was inconvenienced by the building of the canal.

They were deeply political. Canal companies had to buy the favour of landowners to support the canal's construction and the more powerful the landowner, the grander the architectural structure that was promised. And it didn't just stop at bridges. If you ever get the chance, go and visit Tixall Wide on the Staffordshire & Worcestershire Canal. The owners of the hall would only consent to the building of the cut if the engineers would agree to make it look like a beautiful lake – just so that it didn't spoil their view. Oh, the power of money, eh?

There are many types of bridges along the canal: lift bridges, swing bridges, and my favourite, snake bridges, but some bridges have stories all of their own.

BRIDGE 39

There is a famous bridge on the Shropshire Union Canal that is the scene of a very curious tale indeed, and that is Bridge 39. The story goes that in mid-winter 1879, an old farm worker was employed by a well-to-do merchant to take his luggage and that of his friends from Renton in Staffordshire to Woodcock in Shropshire. He loaded the cart with the many luggage cases and strapped them down to make sure that they were secure, harnessed the horse and set off on what he thought would be a fairly uneventful journey.

The road was kind to him all the way to Woodcock and he unloaded the luggage in good time, in fact, such good time that he took the decision to rest for a while before turning around for the journey home. However, the man forgot the time and, before he knew it, the sun was low in the sky and he was facing the thought of travelling in the dark. At around ten o'clock and with a horse so tired it could just about crawl, he came to the high road where it crosses the Birmingham & Liverpool Canal – Bridge 39.

Just as he crossed the bridge, out of nowhere a strange black creature with great white, wild eyes sprang out of the hedgerow and leaped upon the horse's back. The poor animal was so frightened that it forgot all about the long journey on its legs and set off at a gallop over the bridge and down the road.

The old man tried his best to whip the beast off his horse, but the whip just passed straight through its body. He couldn't believe his eyes and his mouth hung open in disbelief. The terrifying journey went on for some time and the man hung on for dear life when, as suddenly as it had arrived, the beast was gone, leaving the man and the horse terrified.

Later that night, he stopped at an inn at Woodseaves and told his tale to any who would listen. In fact, one man was so frightened by the thought of meeting the beast that he opted to stay in the safety of the inn rather than test his courage crossing the bridge.

⊛

The tale above seems to be the most commonly accepted turn of events but what's great about stories is that, somewhere along the way, they get twisted and added to, so here's a couple more that we uncovered, and I think help add to the legend.

OLD JOHNNY

George Benson was a wind-up merchant. That is to say, what he loved to do, more than anything else in the world, was to tell stories. But not your happy-ever-after type of stories. No, what George Benson enjoyed was telling stories that would have you frightened of things that went bump in the night and checking under your bed before you went off to sleep. And he was good at it.

He would start off simple, like just a 'have you heard about' or a 'did you hear what happened', and then he'd wait for the right listener to come and ask, 'Heard what,

George?' And that was it, he had you. It was just a big game to George Benson, and he loved it.

Luckily, most people who had found themselves at the business end of one of George's wind-ups had grown wise to it and you would often hear the words, 'Yeah, yeah, George. Pull the other one!' when he was around. But there was one person who George could wind up again and again and again and that was his best mate, Old Johnny.

Old Johnny was a boatman and he and George had worked boats for a haulage company for years, up and down the Shropshire Union and sometimes further afield. They were good mates, probably due to the fact they were so very different. George talked a lot, whereas Old Johnny, he liked to sit and listen. George had a quick wit but Old Johnny took his time to work out the meaning behind a joke. George was short of stature and Old Johnny was as tall as a bean pole; he had to bend low to get inside the cabin of a boat. But it worked, and whenever they could, they would moor near to each other and have a pint and a smoke so that George could talk and Old Johnny could listen.

Well, George had wound Old Johnny up about all manner of things and each time he fell for it, and it didn't seem to matter how elaborate or simple the story was or how often he did it, Old Johnny was taken in, to the point where it almost got boring and George thought about giving up the game. However, one evening while he was sat in the pub, he overheard a conversation between two old boaters, who were on a nearby table. It made his ears prick up and his mind started to whirl – George Benson had what he thought was the perfect wind-up for his old comrade.

Every boater who worked the Shropshire Union Canal had heard the story of the beast at Bridge 39 and there were all manner of explanations going around as to what, or indeed who, the beast might be, but to this day no one had either met the beast or could prove any of the stories to be true. George timed it to perfection, he knew that in a couple of days' time they were going to be taking their boats up near the area in question and so he made sure that the journey took just long enough so that at the end of the day they had to moor up in view of the bridge. That evening, as Old Johnny and George Benson sat together on a couple of stools by the side of the cut, their backs leaning on George's boat, he started to plant the seeds.

'You'll never guess what I heard,' he said. 'I heard that two weeks ago there were a travelling animal show in the local area full of all manner of exotic stuff. I heard it was a tremendous thing to see, creatures from all over the world, there was, apparently. You would have loved that, you would, Old Johnny!'

'Aye, I would that,' replied Old Johnny. 'Tell me more.'

'Well, apparently,' George continued, in a hushed tone, 'the show was somewhere up near Madeley Wood, you know, near Salop? They'd done the show, to a great big crowd and it comes to the finale, that's the ending bit, you know, and they bring on this big cage covered in a big red sack.' George was starting to warm up and Old Johnny, he was hooked on every word. 'This showman fella, he's harping on about travelling to the jungles of Africa, or some such place, and they've captured this monster and it's right under the cloth. Well anyway, by all accounts, there's this big drum roll and off comes the cloth, and when the crowd see what's under it and in the cage there's screaming and crying and people fainting and what not!'

'What was it, George? What did they see under the cloth?'

'It were a beast, a horrible beast! Apelike, it was, and gigantic like, but it didn't end there. No, that's not the worst of it! As they're watching, them that's not fainted or run away, they're watching the beast and it stretches out its great big hairy arms and rips the door of the cage right off. Well, as you can imagine, everyone wants out of there as quick as a flash and there's a right commotion. The beast escapes, and no one can catch it because it's so strong and terrible. Since then, the beast has been running amok causing fear and distress all across the area and it's been sighted by trusted folk like clergymen and police alike.'

At this point in the tale, Old Johnny's eyes were open wide with horror and his mouth hung open and George could see the cogs going round in his mind until eventually he pieced it all together and said, 'Hang on, George, that's Bridge 39 up there – that's where there was a beast that was said to haunt the place and attack people passing by! But I thought that was just a story to frighten people and it was ages ago, you don't think that this is that old story coming true?'

'I reckon so, Old Johnny, I reckon so. And they say that the beast is probably trying to find somewhere to lay low where no one would think to look for it. They say it's desperate because people are hunting it and there's a reward for getting your hands on it, see. So, I don't know about you, Old Johnny, but I'm going to make sure I keep my cabin locked up real well tonight, just in case, and I've a mind that I won't be getting much sleep until we are well away from Bridge 39!'

George could see the pictures of horror growing in Old Johnny's mind, they were illustrated by the expressions on his face, and on the inside he chuckled away to himself. It was still early evening and the sun hadn't quite set, and he watched as Old Johnny made up his mind. He jumped up and said, 'I'm off!' and George knew that he was going to rush back to his boat and start barricading himself in for the night and would then sit until morning came, listening to every sound.

George Benson sat for an hour, finishing his ale and having a last smoke while the sun slowly dropped over the distant hills. As he sat there, he started to think back over the many times he had put his best friend into a terrible state over the years and he began to feel sorry about it all. He suddenly had images of Old Johnny curled up in the corner of his cabin, eyes wide open, ears straining, hands clutching the fire iron ready to fend off any beast of the night and he became racked with guilt. He made the decision to go up to Old Johnny's boat and put him out of his misery, hoping that his old friend would forgive him, and they could have a good laugh about it. So he set off up the cut in the dark.

When he arrived at Old Johnny's boat, the scene set George Benson's heart racing. The boatman's cabin doors were wide open and there was no sign of Old Johnny. To his horror, there were signs of a struggle inside; blankets and other items were strewn over the floor. George couldn't believe his eyes and he started to have a little panic. What could have happened to his oldest and best friend? His mind started back to the story he had overheard in the pub just a few days before, which he was sure was just that, a story, but suddenly here he was, at Bridge 39 and Old Johnny had been taken in the night by a great hairy beast to who knows where.

George Benson panicked, and he ran, tears streaming down his face, back to his boat. He had it in his mind to close the door and in the safety of the cabin hatch a plan to escape. However, when he arrived, something was wrong. The cabin doors were wide open – he was certain that he had closed them – and as he carefully peered into the gloom, he saw it. There, by the dying glow of his fire, he could make out the shape of a great hulking beast. It was covered in hair all over its back and it seemed to take up all the space in the cabin, from the floor to the ceiling, but with its back to George, it hadn't noticed him.

Well, his heart was nearly jumping out of his chest as thoughts of what the beast might do to him if it were to catch him ran through his mind, and so he ran, up and down the cut, and as he ran, he called for help. He banged on sides of other boats and shouted, 'Beast! Beast! Help, there's a beast!' Out from their boats came other people and they followed George in a hurry.

When George could see he had a crowd, he gathered them close and quickly recounted the night's events. Slowly, now, and cautiously, they went, George leading the way back to his boat, and they all peered to see the beast inside. George stretched out a hand to open the hatch door wider when, without warning, the beast started to unwind itself and with a great 'ROAR!' it leaped and caught hold of George's outstretched hand. George let out a scream the likes of which he hadn't made since he was a small child, and while the beast still held him firmly by the wrist, he lay in a ball on the ground and whimpered words that none could hear, until eventually he noticed that nothing more terrible than being grabbed had happened ...

Slowly, George Benson opened his eyes. The first thing he noticed was the grinning face of his friend, Old Johnny beaming down at him. The second thing he noticed was that it was Old Johnny who was holding his wrist so tight. Finally, he heard the growing laughter that spread throughout the chattered crowd. As Old Johnny lifted George to his feet, he gave his friend a few moments to take it all in and to calm himself down and then eventually he spoke. 'You see, it's not just you, George, who can tell stories and play jokes. Everyone here has been on the end of one of your wind-ups at one time or another and, well, I know it's taken awhile for me to put this one together but we all thought that you could do with a taste of your own medicine, just so you can see what it feels like once in a while. I hope that you will see the funny side of it one day and that you might think twice in future before you use people's fears against them for your fun!'

Well, I heard that George did, eventually, see the funny side of what happened and that he did, almost, change his ways. He still liked to have a joke with his friends, every now and again, but the one thing that never changed for George Benson was that every time he passed through Bridge 39, he felt a little shiver of fear from the memory of that night and it never left him, just like the story of the beast of Bridge 39 has never gone away.

It's often the thing with stories, we think of them as old things. Well, the beast of Bridge 39 is far from that. There have been more recent encounters reported, as you are about to find out. Now, I know what you're going to say when you read it, you're going to say, '1980s? That's not recent, Ian!' Well, it's recent enough to make me think twice about heading down the Shroppie, so off you go, dear friend, read on.

A Modern Mystery

Sometime during the 1980s – the story doesn't get any more precise than that – a young family decided to take a boating holiday. Their plan was to travel along the Shropshire Union for a number of days, try to get as far as they could, and then stop somewhere quiet for a couple of days before turning and heading back.

The journey that they were on was set to send them under Bridge 39, but none of the family were aware that it meant anything, as they hadn't heard the story that you have, you see. Well, on the morning of day two they set off early, wanting to get as long a day travelling as they could, as they had spotted on the map what looked like a really nice place to moor up, if they could get there by the end of the day.

All was going well and at lunchtime the husband took the tiller so that his wife could go inside to get some lunch set out. The sun was ahead of him, and he had to shade his eyes against the light, but he suddenly became aware of a figure staring down at him from the top of the Bridge 39.

To his horror, as the bridge came closer, he could tell that this was no man at all. It was a strange creature, covered from head to foot in coarse, black hair. It had large, maddened eyes and was staring right at him. The figure suddenly dipped down behind the ridge of the bridge and, fearing that the creature was making its way to the towpath, he put the engine in full throttle. He hit the boat off both sides of the bridge, and could hear metal scraping on stone and shrieks from inside the boat as people and property were thrown about from the impact. The man didn't care, he just wanted to be away from the scene, and he pushed the boat hard, not daring to look back.

When he could finally speak about it, the man told the story a number of times over the next few days, first to his family and eventually to the local police. When the man recounted what had happened to the police officer, he calmly said to the man that it was really nothing to worry about and it was just the monkey man who haunted the bridge ever since an old boatman had drowned in the cut, many years before.

And that's all I've got to tell you about Bridge 39.

We have, of course, our own bridge story and it goes like this. A number of years ago, we were taking *Hawker*, not down the Shropshire Union, but up through Manchester, towards the Pennines for the summer, when we came across a lift bridge. I got off the boat to open it, windlass in hand, only to find that it was a hydraulic lift, the first one I'd ever come across.

Well, the lift was part of a fairly busy city road, so once I had worked out how to operate it, I set to, keen to get us through and not hold up the traffic. The alarms sounded as I pushed the open button. Barriers dropped to stop cars and wagons and the lift went up, and once it was fully opened, Jo pushed the throttle and got *Hawker* safely through.

And that's when disaster struck. The bridge wouldn't close. I tried everything, honest. The traffic line got longer and longer, but nothing worked. It wasn't long before I was joined by a number of very irate blokes wearing football shirts, some blue and some red, who very kindly informed me that the tailback both ways was now a mile long and it was Derby Day. Did I realise what I was doing to the football fans of Manchester?

I was going to point out that I was a Liverpool supporter, but thought better of it and rang the engineers instead. Confident that I had done all that I could, I slowly made my apologies and we set off down the cut, thinking, 'Well, at least they were angry with me and not each other, for once.'

United lost, by the way, but the bridge was working again the next day, so all's well that ends well.

About the Horses

You really can't have a book of stories about narrow-boats without talking horses – they were the engine of the times and a boatman's best friend. Before steam and diesel, the horse was king. And because of this, the boatmen treated them as such, even going so far as to have special feed mixes made up for their horses and kept as family secrets.

Horses were used, of course, before the waterways were created but the road conditions at the end of the eighteenth century were poor, to say the least. Suddenly, with the frictionless travel that the canals had to offer, horses could pull ten times more weight than by land.

It took two people to run a horse-drawn boat: one to walk the horse and the other to work the tiller and keep the boat in deep water. In an ideal world, there would be a third to set the locks but that's where having a few children came in useful. I've yet to see a horse-drawn boat on the cut and I'm sure when one day I do, it will take my breath away, but maybe in the age we live in, what with the way our climate is changing, the days of seeing horses pulling boats throughout our country might just come once again.

THE DAFT BOATMAN

It was an autumn evening around twilight time, when the light makes it hard to tell the way things really are, when an old collier from the local mine emerged from underground after finishing his shift. Well, the old boy had worked a long stint at the seam and had a mind to clear his thoughts and his lungs by taking in the cool night air. And so he set off towards home, the long way round, by taking a snicket through the hedges and on to the Staffordshire & Worcestershire Canal.

It was a way that he was well used to and even though the light was very quickly failing he began just ambling along without a care, watching the still water and letting his mind wander. But as he immersed himself into his surroundings, he became increasingly aware that all was not right. Up ahead of him, off in the darkness, there was a strange sound, the sound of metal scraping against stone, and as his ears became more alert, he began to determine the unmistakable sounds of a man hard at work, the curses confirming that whoever this was and whatever they were about it was none too agreeable to the individual.

The collier slowed his pace so that he could take in the scene and noticed that up ahead there was a bridge, but something was blocking the way and, as he got closer still, he could see that it was an old working boat stopped in the bridge hole with its horse stood stock still next to it. Well, by itself that's not an unusual sight because a bridge hole is a good enough place to halt if you need to nip into your cabin to make a brew – the bridge opening stops your boat drifting, you see? But the strangest sight of all was the answer to the scraping sound, the boatman was chiselling away at the underside of the stone bridge and the words coming off him can't be put into print.

Curious and amused, the old collier approached the scene and gently, so as to not startle the boatman, he asked the fella what the problem could be and why was he scraping away at the top of the bridge arch?

The boatman stopped his work for a second, probably glad of the rest, and looked our friend up and down. Finally, after what felt like an age, he offered an explanation. 'It's the horse," he said. 'She's a good strong horse and has always done me well, but as I've come further north the bridges have got lower and she won't go through as she dunt like to scrape her ears on the stone. So, here's me cutting two grooves with this chisel for the horse's ears to go through and I can carry on my journey in haste.'

Well, there in the darkness, the two men stepped back a moment to weigh up the job in hand. The miner could see how little and slow the progress was as the boatman had hardly made a mark on the old, cold stone and so, if only to muffle a laugh, he offered a simple solution. 'I know a thing or two about shifting earth and muck and soil and I can see that the ground beneath your feet is far softer than the stone above your head and so might it be quicker to go get a shovel off the back of yon boat and take out a layer of the tow path? That will lower the ground a little and is sure to let the horse move through.'

A silence settled on the space for a moment as the boatman contemplated this advice, but then he turned to his new friend and with a very serious look, replied, 'Well, what help would that be? It's the horse's ears that are too tall for the roof not her legs that are too long for the floor!' And without another word, he returned to his thankless task.

Well, the collier, he stood for a moment in silence and then muttered the old adage, 'There's nowt so queer as folk', and left the daft boatman to his labour. Soon he was back home with his feet up by the fire, laughing to himself and concluding that it takes all sorts to turn the world, and it does indeed.

Poor Old Horse

A number one came a bacca-ring by,
And they think so, and they hope so.
I said, Old man, that horse will die.
Oh, poor old horse!

Oh, he'll work all night and he'll work all day,
And they say so, and they hope so.
Put him on the inside he'll back her away.
Oh, poor old horse!

(Part of a traditional song known to boatmen. To 'bacca' is to let a horse walk alone while the driver has a smoke.)

BARNETT'S BREACH

Ted Newsum never knew the high life, nor did he ever want it. He was, and always had been, happy with his lot. He was born to a poor boat family from Wolverhampton. In fact, he was born on the very boat that he now owned, handed down to him by his father. *Starlight*, she was called – 60ft long with a strong wooden hull that had done many a mile in its life. Before Ted was born and when *Starlight* was young, his father had pulled the boat himself, with a leather haulage strap across his broad chest and attached by rope to the boat mast. He would drag *Starlight* from job to job, with Ted's mother on the tiller. You see, they just didn't have the means to afford a horse to do the work.

When Ted came along, it put extra pressure on the family and things at times were bleak. But worry not, this is a story of hope, not despair, because Ted grew up quick and strong and it wasn't too long before he was a useful hand on board the boat. In time, with three of them now to carry the load, Ted's father was able to start to put a little bit by, job by job, until the day came that he had the money to buy the beast they needed.

Ted's dad bought a cob, and a good strong one at that. Not too big for the low bridges and with a steady temperament, she was the perfect choice. Ted was quick to learn the ropes and the cob was as quick to understand when to pull and when to let the boat have its way and so now, they could move twice as fast.

And for a good few years that's what happened, and things went well for them, but you know, the years of dragging and toil at the tiller for long hours had taken it out of Ted's mother and father and eventually enough was enough. The day came that they could do no more and they handed the boat to their son.

As sad as he was, Ted was a young man and loyal and he took to the task as he was asked. In fact, he made a go of it, did Ted. He took on a chap to help, at first, and then he caught the eye of a young boating woman who eventually became his wife, and *Starlight* became their home, just as it had been for his mum and dad. But then, just as things were going from strength to strength, tragedy struck.

Ted's mum, who was full of years, passed away. Well, his dad couldn't be without her and followed a few days later and Ted was beside himself with grief. But it didn't stop there, the old cob who had dragged that boat from job to job went lame and so had to be put out of her misery. Ted and his wife hit rock bottom.

However, there was some light at the end of the tunnel for Ted, and it might sound a bit funny where the light came from when I tell you, but after the cost of laying his parents in the ground and doing the best for the old cob, he worked out that at a push they had enough money to buy themselves a new beast to pull the boat. He felt that, in some way, by doing this – by making sure that they didn't go back to the old ways of pulling by manpower alone – he was honouring the memory of his parents. His wife understood, what with her being off the boats as well, and so off he went to auction.

Times had moved on somewhat from when his old dad was last there, as had the price of things, and when Ted came back home that day, his wife could hardly believe what she saw. The night before the auction, the two of them had sat by the stove and dreamed about a new cob or maybe a shire, but never in her memory of the conversation did she recall talking about a mule. But that's what Ted held in his hands, and a sad example of one at that. Well, she was about to give Ted her thoughts on the matter when he spoke first and told her that he couldn't believe the price. There was not a horse there that day that their money would stretch to and the mule was all they could afford. But, he said, the man who sold him the mule had told him that if he treated it right, this mule was the best beast of burden any man could wish for.

And so, true to his word, that's exactly what Ted did. He worked with that mule like it was a friend. He was patient and caring, he cleaned its hooves and fed it well, taught it all he could and, do you know, the man that sold the mule to Ted had spoken the truth – that mule was the finest beast that anyone could wish for and stronger than any horse that Ted or his wife had ever seen.

But they were a strange sight on the cut among the cobs and shire horses. The mule looked like a poor relation and people laughed at Ted and his wife as they ambled by. To Ted it was like water off a duck's back but sadly, not to his wife. She hated that people poked fun and it really started to get to her, being talked about behind her back, and eventually she had to speak to Ted about it.

The day that she plucked up the courage to speak to her husband was 9 September 1899, a day that neither she nor Ted would forget. She had decided that at the end of the day when they moored up and had tended to the mule, she would sit him down and tell him how she felt and that if he loved her, and she was sure that he did, he would find a way to replace the mule with something more socially acceptable. She was nervous about what he would say because she knew her husband and, although most would describe him as a practical man, he also had feelings and cared for the mule a lot.

It was around 4 p.m., and they had just made their way steadily passed the Rattlechain and Stour Valley Brick Works on the Birmingham Canal when, unbeknownst to them, there was a bank breach just behind them. The breach was bad and this wasn't just a seepage. A 6-mile stretch of water was now thundering through the gap and down into the brick works, causing a huge amount of damage.

All of this went unnoticed by Ted and his wife, they just ambled along minding their own business. But as the draft of the water flow got stronger, Ted noticed that the old mule was starting to strain and the ropes tethered to the mule's tackle were starting to creak, Ted turned to look to his wife at the tiller and could see that she was worried and looking behind herself, trying to shout towards Ted. The noise of the water was suddenly so loud her voice couldn't be heard. Ted urged the mule on and ran back along the cut to see the problem and once he saw the breach, he knew how much trouble they were in. Where the bank had broken away was a steep bank to the brick works and if *Starlight* was dragged down, his wife would be away with it.

In desperation, Ted sprinted back along the cut to find his mule at a standstill, the pull of the water was so strong even the mule's sturdy muscles could not move the boat. A crowd was gathering, and all stood with mouths open, not knowing what to do.

They could really see only one chance and that was to cut the ropes and hope that the boat hit the canal bottom before it reached the breach. Ted stopped for a second and looked at the crowd of boatmen, almost able to read their minds. All of them had laughed at Ted at one time or another. He looked back at his wife, who clung on to the tiller unable to help, and then at his mule, and, in that moment, he knew what he had to do.

Ted went to the side of the beast and he started to talk to it, right into its ear. Nobody could hear a word he said but they could see how calm he was, how much he trusted that mule, his friend. And the mule, it listened, and it was, said people watching, like the mule took strength from Ted's words. It suddenly strained, and its muscles tightened. They watched it lean into the tackle and goodness knows how it moved, slowly at first, but building. It moved first one hoof then the next, with all the time Ted whispering in the mule's ear. Forward, one step at a time, heart pounding, the beast that everyone had doubted proved itself above any horse on the cut. It pulled and pulled, until eventually it cleared the draft, and the boat was suddenly free of its pull.

Ted stopped talking and pulled with the mule until the boat and his wife were safe. The crowd cheered and gathered round to congratulate Ted and his wife, but especially the mule.

The water on the 6-mile stretch eventually drained and miraculously, even though three boats were pulled through the breach, no one was seriously hurt. The rebuilding of the breach took some time and the stranded boats and their owners had to be compensated for the loss of earnings.

The blame finally landed on the doorstep of Mr Barnett, the owner of the brick works itself. Apparently, he had weakened the bank on purpose to cause the damage to his works and claim insurance, but it ended up costing him dearly, including a prison sentence.

As for Ted, he was just glad of a rest – as was the mule – and do you know, his wife never did have that conversation with him about changing the beast.

⊕

Thankfully, breaches are few and far between, but they do still happen and just like the last tale, it's often people messing about with things that they should leave well alone that causes the bother. On 15 March 2018, a mile of the Middlewich branch of the busy Shropshire Union was left empty, stranding twenty boats. A 70ft hole appeared in the canal bank. It had collapsed and the water in the mile stretch rushed through and into the river below. One boat was so close to the hole that it was very nearly taken through by the flood, and apparently there was someone sleeping on the boat at the time.

The actual cause of the breach was that all four paddles on the lock above had been left open, most likely by vandals, and the excess water had led to overflowing on a low bit of the embankment. The overflow continued, washing away more and more material and so the hole appeared. Jo and I went to see the breach and I couldn't believe my eyes, seeing that enormous space where water and boats should have been.

In the following few days, they managed to re-float most of the boats and 10,000 fish were rescued from the remaining puddle at the bottom of the canal. It cost £3 million to repair the breach and the canal finally reopened at the end of December 2019.

In some places along the canal, the lock mechanisms have anti-vandal locks fitted to stop people doing exactly what is described above. They are a right pain and can really slow your journey down, but when I saw the breach, it did make me think again about my various rants that I've had over the years.

ABOUT THE PILFERING

By the middle of the nineteenth century it was common practice for a lot of boatmen to pilfer the goods that they were employed to carry. What made the risk worth taking was the fact that there were a lot of people in our towns and cities who were prepared to receive the stolen goods. And the boatmen were good at the task, even going so far as to have special tools made so that they could open caskets and barrels, siphon off a share of the contents, replace the weight with something worthless and make it look like nothing had been tampered with. Many a time a tavern landlord would tap and spile a cask of ale, only to find that he was serving dirty canal water.

Jo tells me that someone told her, if a boat was transporting chocolate the children on board would pilfer bits and add it to a mug of hot water to make hot chocolate. She thinks that this is how it was invented in the first place but we're not sure if it's true.

Some boats went as far as smuggling. Hidden spaces were cleverly created in the hulls of the boats to allow them to carry contraband undetected. And nothing seemed to put them off. Arrests were made on regular occasions but the plucky boatmen just shrugged it off and continued with their deeds. I've come to the conclusion that if I had been alive back then, I would have most definitely been a smuggler – and a really good one, at that!

THE WRONG BARREL

The boats that ran the inland waterways during the industrial period of our country would carry all manner of goods to feed the needs of the growing populations of our towns and cities. And it was taken as normal practice for the people who ran the boats to help themselves to small quantities of the cargo as they travelled long journeys throughout the land. For instance, if your boat was carrying coal, then to stoke your fire that night with a few shovels of your cargo wouldn't affect your load and weight that much, so no harm was done. However, sometimes some boaters went too far – too far by a long way – as this story will tell.

One fine summer's morning, the crew of *Bee*, a 70ft wooden-hull narrowboat, left Paddington in the early hours, weighed down with all manner of goods, including rum, brandy and gunpowder. The day had all the signs of being a hot one and that was even before the sun was over the horizon.

The three men who ran *Bee* had worked the boat for many years and knew her and each other well. All three had their jobs to do and they did it with ease, as those who know their jobs are able to do. However, as the heat of the day grew, so did a thought in each of the men's heads, and that thought was ale.

Well, they just about managed to work on until lunchtime before the heat of the sun had done its work and the men could resist no longer. They all knew what was waiting in the back cabin of the boat. It was a firkin of beer that was just about talking to them.

They drove a pin into the towpath and put the boat on the mooring ropes and poured out three mugs of the cool ale. This was all good and well, and there was no harm in it. However, the drinking didn't stop there, the men's thirst was so big, and the sun was so hot that they continued to drink as they worked.

As night fell, the barrel ran dry but the men's thirst had not been quenched and so they tied the boat up outside one of the many inns that offered a hearty welcome along the way and continued their merry making. But, as they sat there in the corner of the inn, conversation turned to their cargo and why they were spending their own money when there was a stronger and much cheaper alternative on board. They agreed to forsake some of their cargo and have a go at the rum.

The three men left the inn, untied *Bee* and quietly pulled her through the still water, so as not disturb anybody, and finally moored up in the dark not too far away from a remote farm. They knew their business, and armed with nothing but an axe and a small lamp they unhooked the canvas hold cover and climbed inside and set about attacking a barrel, looking forward to a mug of the strong stuff.

Well, strong it was, because although the lamp wasn't that good at giving off light, enough to read the signage on the barrel, it was good enough to provide a spark. The blast that erupted from the gunpowder barrel blew the boat to pieces, set fire to the farm sheds and finally put an end to the boaters' thirst.

❧

This next story has a special place in my heart, I think it was probably the first real folk story that I heard, and I was very young when I heard it, although I don't remember who told it to me. My cousins lived in Slaithwaite when I was a kid, so we spent a fair bit of time up there when I was young and I loved the place. My brother, Andrew, and me practically learned to swim in the nearby Sparf reservoir. Our dad told us that there was a killer pike under the water so if we didn't swim quick enough it would bite our feet off. (That kind of educational approach was common where I grew up and goes a long way to explaining how I have turned out as I have.) Lastly, it's the underlying politics of the story that I like. I'm sure you will understand as you read it.

MOON RAKERS

The early 1800s was a turbulent time. Britain was at war with France and Napoleon was threatening to invade England at any moment and so, to pay for the defence of our island, the government raised the tax level, which sent many people across the country into poverty. In the mill towns of the North of England there were added pressures. Mill owners were forced to bring down the price of cloth production and increase productivity to support the war efforts, and the only way to do this was to change the way that they paid their workers and change the way that cloth was produced, and that meant mechanisation.

Skilled workers soon found themselves out of work, their labour replaced by machines that could do the same job at twice the rate and a fraction of the cost. Their only option to provide for their families was to go to war and many, sadly, never returned.

But for others, the war was not on foreign soil and the enemy wasn't the French. Many in the mill towns saw the introduction of machines to the workplace as a political move against the working classes; just another way for the aristocracy to get richer and to hell with the poor. So they began to fight back.

A story started to spread of a man called King Ludd, who was rallying his own army of working men and striking back against the fat-cat mill owners. It was said that King Ludd had smashed mill machines in Nottingham single-handed and now lived as an outlaw in Sherwood Forest.

Well, whether the story was true or not, King Ludd lit a fire in the hearts of many people and the Luddite movement was born. All across the North of England cloth workers revolted, machines were smashed, mills were burnt, and mill owners feared for their lives. So much so, that the government had to step in. Laws were quickly passed that made machine-breaking a crime punishable by death, but this deterred nothing and very few arrests were made. Luddite activists lived in very close communities and neighbours would not give up neighbours.

Eventually, the problem became so bad that the government had to send militia from the South to try and police the areas affected. The militia men were given full licence to use whatever means necessary to bring the Luddites to justice. The movement was driven underground, meetings to arrange mill attacks took place in secret locations and information was passed from person to person in ways that only those who needed to know would understand.

'But what has this got to do with the canals?' I hear you cry. Well, in a small village called Slaithwaite, near Huddersfield in the West Riding of Yorkshire, there was a big militia presence. There had been a lot of Luddite activity in the area and rumour had it that a large mill in the neighbouring village of Marsden was going to be attacked. The militia didn't know when it would happen, but they knew it would, and so they were on high alert, especially at night time.

In Slaithwaite there lived a man by the name of Tim Brig. He was 'Slawit' born and bred, and owned an inn just off the Huddersfield narrow canal. Well, as I said, times were hard and there was very little money going round so Tim Brig saw his business slowly die. However, Tim, like most of the folk of the West Riding, was not the kind of man to sit idle and so he came to an arrangement with the many boatmen who transported cloth from the mills, down the valley and eventually out to the ports like Liverpool. The boatmen could get their hands on all manner of goods that hadn't been seen by the eyes of officials and so they brought Tim Brig barrels of rum and brandy and they sold it to him cheap – and that, of course, made it cheap for his customers, and as long as no one told the militia, everyone was a winner.

The arrangement was simple. So as not to attract attention, the boatmen as they passed would moor up near the inn and, as they drank their fill, Tim would slip them money. Then, as they went on their way, they would travel under the low bridge near the inn, secure the barrels out of sight as close to the sun going down as possible and then, under cover of darkness, Tim Brig and a few trusted men would use a couple of old rakes to pull the barrels to the canal side and have them away to the cellars. This was something that was done once a week.

All was well for quite some time and the arrangement suited everyone. Tim Brig's inn was a busy little place, until one night things almost came to a very abrupt end.

A boat came through as arranged, one late afternoon. Money exchanged hands and Tim made arrangements to meet his men later that evening to rake the barrels, but as the boatmen left they warned Tim that there was a full moon out that night and doing business that you don't want people to see under a full moon was bad luck.

Tim Brig was not a rash man and he would take advice when it was given in good faith, and he thought long and hard about the boatmen's warning. However, the barrels in his cellar were almost dry and with full ones waiting for him, he decided to take the risk.

Later that evening, as most people slept in their beds, Tim and his men set off into the darkness. They left the inn by the back door, made sure that the drop to the cellar was unlocked so that there would be no hold-up later, checked to see that no one was around and then headed off to the cut.

It was a clear night, the valley hills black against the starry sky, and the moon was about as bright a moon that the men had ever seen. They were very exposed even under the cover of night. As they approached the water, Tim could see that the light of the moon hitting the water sent it silver and the canal was so still he could see the face of the moon in all its beautiful detail.

He had to shake himself to bring his attention back to business. They were at the bridge and as they looked into its dark entrance, they could make out the shape of the barrels bobbing on the surface of the water. Tim hitched up the back of his coat so that one of the other men could grab a hold of his belt. He could then use both hands to work the rake and lean into the bridge opening without fear of falling into the cold water.

He stretched out with the rake to gather the rope that was holding the barrels together and was just about to pull them to the bank when suddenly there was a shout above them. The men's hearts nearly leaped from their chests.

As quick as they could, the three men pulled away from the water's edge and stood in silence, side by side, to see what would happen next. In less than a minute, they were surrounded by militia, a band of around fifty men, all armed and all looking very dangerous. Tim was suddenly aware that he was shivering, and it felt like an age before anyone said a word.

One of the militia men stepped towards them and looked them up and down. These men weren't local, Tim could see it in their faces, and when the man spoke his accent was strange and drawn out, although Tim understood every word. The man wanted to know what their business was and where they were off to. Why were they carrying tools? He asked if they were Ludd's men and then described what would happen to them if they didn't choose their words carefully.

The three men stood there in a blind panic. Words wouldn't come to their lips and as they hesitated, unable to explain, the militia started to close in. Tim knew in his heart that things were about to get very painful for the three of them unless one of them spoke, and that's when it came to him, like a light coming on in his mind.

'It's a tragedy,' said Tim. 'A tragedy of the worst kind. Me and my friends here were just taking a stroll after a long night's work, when we found ourselves down here by the cut. Well, that's when we saw her and it troubled us deeply. Hasn't the moon herself fallen out of the sky in all her majesty and dropped down into the canal?'

The militia stood listening with open mouths, so Tim continued. 'Well, what were we to do, we said to each other? We couldn't stand by and let her drift off to Lancashire, so we ran to the inn where we keep rakes and we've come back, and as you can see, lads, this is us trying desperately to rake the moon out of the water, because

❧

no one in their right mind – not even the moon – would want to go to Lancashire!'

At the end of the speech, Tim Brig stood quiet, a look of simple honesty on his face. The militia men stood in silence, looking from one to another, until eventually the captain of the men stepped towards Tim. He looked him carefully up and down and then very simply patted him on the shoulder like an owner would a dog and then ordered his men to move off, leaving Tim and his friends to carry on their business.

As the militia walked away from the scene, they questioned the captain as to why he had left them to their job. He simply replied that before he had come North, he'd been warned that the people up here had very strange ways, some that no man could understand, and it was obvious that those three were muddled in their heads.

෴

There never was an attack on the mill at Marsden, although some days later the owner was killed in a Luddite attack. After that, the militia came down hard on anyone suspected of illegal activity and the Luddite rebellion was brought to an end. But three things survived from those days. Firstly, the name of Tim Brigg – the humped bridge in Slaithwaite still goes by that name, so that's him immortalised forever. Secondly, the term 'moonraker', which can be claimed by anyone that comes from that beautiful little village in the West

Riding of Yorkshire. Thirdly, and by no means the least, it's the story – the story has survived and now you have it, so please tell it to anyone you think might need a good tale.

ABOUT A PORT

When I first thought about trying to put together a collection of canal stories, a number of people said, 'Good luck!'. The general consensus being that most of the information available was merely anecdotal or historical. It was, as ever it is, my wife Jo who said we should contact the Canal & River Trust at Ellesmere Port and see if we could look at their archive.

It turned out to be the best thing we could have done. The place is a treasure trove of information and the staff couldn't do enough to help. We stayed in Ellesmere for a number of days, so we had a chance to have a good look around. You don't have to go far to get a sense of how important the place was as a site where canal meets sea.

Ellesmere Port was named after what was once the 'Ellesmere Canal'. It was originally intended to join three rivers, the Mersey, Dee and Severn, but the Severn link never did get completed and eventually the Ellesmere Canal was renamed the Shropshire Union, linking North Wales and it's precious mineral supplies with the industrial towns and cities that needed them. Much later, the Manchester Ship Canal was built, when the tradesmen of Manchester wanted better access to the ships docking in Liverpool.

Just walking off the narrow canal and onto the ship canal is enough to make you realise how vulnerable a narrowboat would feel, as I hope you sense from the story below. The following words are part of a song printed in a Preston paper between 1847 and 1849:

Seaport Town of Manchester

Oh dear! Oh dear! this a curious age is,
Alterations all the rage is,
Old and young in the stream are moving,
All in the general cry improving,
To Manchester there's news come down, sirs,
They're going to make it a seaport town, sir,
Nought you'll see but ships and sailors.

Thus 'twill be I'll bet you a crown sir,
When Manchester's a sea-port town sir,

When the first ship appears in sight,
The town will be all joy and delight;
Eating, drinking, dancing, singing,
And th' old church bells will crack with ringing,
They'll cover the bridge with touts and prigs sir,
Aldermen too in their gowns and wigs sir,
The heads of the town with all their forces,
The Manchester Mayor too drawn by horses.

STUCK IN THE LOCK

There was a feeling of nervous tension in the air when, early one September morning, a flotilla of six narrowboats set off from the Albert Dock in Liverpool. Their journey would eventually take them down onto the canal network at Ellesmere Port, but first they had to tackle the great Mersey River and then onto the Manchester Shipping Canal. It was a journey not to be undertaken lightly, especially when you are guaranteed to be the smallest vessels out on the water and you're about to try to navigate a river with notoriously strong tides.

The year was 1930 and carriage by narrowboat was gradually declining. As a consequence, narrowboat owners were having to take any work that was offered to them to make ends meet and so, even though they were anxious about navigating the shipping channels, they were prepared to take on the task.

The boats set off into the main channel of the Mersey in good weather and the tide was running with them so they made good headway, but even though all on board the boats were experienced men and had made the journey many times before, none could shake the sense of awe at the magnitude of the place and the feeling of vulnerability. However, they ploughed on with grim determination until eventually they had made the crossing and sounded their horns to alert the lock workers to open the lock gates that would bring them down on to the shipping canal.

But even this move from river to canal would bring them no relief. The Manchester Ship Canal stretched for 36 miles and had heavy traffic consisting of seafaring ships that still made the narrowboat crews feel vulnerable.

However, the best approach, as they all knew, was to get on with the job in hand.

Such was the size of the great lock that all six boats were able to fit inside at the same time. The crews worked quickly to rope the boats together to stop them from crashing against one another as the water quickly emptied from the lock. Down and down went the boats, the sound was terrific and seemed to take an age. When eventually the lock was emptied, the lock gates opened, and the boats could be untied to allow them to continue their journey.

They entered the shipping canal in single file, eager to get away from its vastness and on to the safe familiarity of the narrow canal. Luckily for them, the distance to the Eastham lock at Ellesmere Port wasn't too great and the men's hearts were lifted as the lock soon came into view. The only down side was that the lock, unlike that of the shipping canal, would only allow one boat at once to descend, so the boats and their crews waited anxiously for the first boat to enter. It was a tense time.

The skipper of the first boat brought the bow forward to allow the crew to jump to the bank and then waited as they opened the lock gates to let the boat in. Once the boat had cleared the gates, the men swung it shut and when the skipper was happy he signalled for them to open the sluice to let the water out and let the boat descend.

But nothing happened. Even though the water dropped from the lock, the boat didn't move, not even an inch. This was bad news and could only mean one thing – the boat must be wedged between the lock walls and if they lost all the water it would leave the boat dangling in mid-air and it could plunge down at any minute.

The skipper gave a cry and quickly his crew could see the problem. As quick as they could they closed the sluice to stop the water and opened the top gate sluice to let more in. Then, once the water was balanced again they alerted the five waiting boats and went to investigate.

The skipper and his crew looked intently around the boat close to the lock walls try to find where the boat had become wedged but they just couldn't understand it. There was a decent gap all around the hull, which meant that the problem must be under the water.

By now, a crowd had gathered to see what the problem was and with the boats still on the shipping canal, the skipper was getting hot under the collar. However, he persevered. Grabbing a bilge hook from the top of the cabin, he started to probe around under the water until, eventually, with a look of confusion, he told everyone that there was something under the boat and they should let the water out to see what it was.

Well, it took some convincing, but eventually they agreed and once again they opened the sluice gate. Water gushed out of the lock, and the boat stayed where it was – but then, to everyone's amazement, the problem revealed itself. Under the boat, holding the entire weight of the steel hull was a 5-ton grampus whale, and it was alive!!

All of a sudden there was a burst of life as the skipper and crew forgot about the perils of river travel and seafaring ships and turned their attention to saving the life of this beautiful creature. They filled the lock, pulled the boat back onto the shipping canal and slowly, with gentle persuasion, coaxed the whale out of the lock. All boat movement on the canal was stopped as the beast swam out into the water, glad to be free of its stone prison.

A message was sent from narrowboat to narrowboat and suddenly those six boats had a purpose. Taking control of the water, they carefully steered the whale back up the Manchester Ship Canal and into the great lock so that it could be taken up and released back into the Mersey River, and hopefully back into the sea.

And do you know? As the whale made its way into the lock, it let rip a 30ft-high spout of water to celebrate and the men on those boats gave out a great cheer in response!

About the Keelmen
and Their Boats

As I came thro' Sandgate,
Thro' Sandgate, thro' Sandgate,
As I came thro' Sandgate,
I heard a lassie sing:

'O, weel may the keel row,
The keel row, the keel row,
O weel may the keel row
That my laddie's in.

'He wears a blue bonnet,
Blue bonnet, blue bonnet,
He wears a blue bonnet
A dimple in his chin.

'And weel may the keel row,
The keel row, the keel row,

And weel may the keel row
That my laddie's in.'

This story takes us away from the canal side for just a little while, but we found this story about the keel-boat families of the north-east and thought that it was too good not to include. The tale takes us to the Sandgate area of the great City of Newcastle upon Tyne, a place that, even to this day, is known for its tight-knit communities and a huge sense of 'looking after your own'.

Keelmen were employed to take coal from the pits further up the River Tyne on keelboats. The boats were made with a shallow draft so that they could work in the low-level waters near the mines. The boats had small sails but could be oared if the wind was too still and the keelmen would transport the coal down the river to larger boats and out to sea.

Keelmen were paid per trip or 'tide' and it was notoriously hard work. Most workers would be unable to continue much beyond the age of 40. The work was passed down from father to son, and the younger man would work as an apprentice until his elder was sure his son could manage the sheer physical task of unloading the boat by hand, as well as being able to handle the keelboat itself.

The keelmen marked themselves out from other working folk by wearing very distinctive clothing. They worked in wide, knee-length breeches and, on a Sunday, they would dress up in their best blue jackets, yellow waistcoats and wide-brimmed hats.

CUDDY ALDER'S GOOSE PIES

In 1683 a girl was born to the Brailsworth family in the Sandgate area of Newcastle upon Tyne. Born to a poor family, the girl's future was already determined. She would spend her life working in servitude until the day she died. However, she would never forget her roots, and as she grew, she became quickly known for her skills with a kitchen cleaver and her fiery temper, something that she had to learn to contain.

At the grand age of 25, the now Mrs Brailsworth came into the service of a man called Cuthbert Alder. Mr Alder was a merchant who lived at Longbenton in the north-east end of the city. He was a very rich and notoriously arrogant man, who was particularly vocal about his views of the lower classes, who were of course the very people upon which his wealth was built.

But it wasn't just his wealth and opinion that Mr Alder was well known for within the company he kept – no, he was also known for the length of his belt or, in other words, he was a very fat man, which could be explained by the size of his well-stocked larder and a particular partiality to a finely cooked goose pie. He had Mrs Brailsworth make and store these in large quantities.

Well, Cuddy Alder had many people working for him because he liked to think of his servants as a show of his status and wealth but of all his employees, Mrs Brailsworth was his most prized for she was the individual who, with her famed skills with her sharp cleaver, plucked, gutted, diced and stuffed the thick buttery crusts that formed the walls, roof and floor of the aforementioned famous pastries. Mrs Brailsworth spent much of her time while around Cuddy Alder biting her tongue.

Life on the opposite side of the city was, however, very different. The living conditions for the majority of working people in the 1700s were desperate and most lived a hand-to-mouth existence. This included the city's keelboat families. Keelboats, short but wide beamed, once ran the coal and goods that fed the industries of our great towns and cities, and it was no different along the rivers Tyne and Wear.

The keelboats were worked by tight-knit communities of men and boys who rarely came ashore at all due to the pressure of trying to make a wage from the heavy work of their trade and the need to support their families. They preferred at night time to lash their boats together to create floating villages, where they would eat, sleep and live.

But in 1709, things came to a head. Conditions for keelboat workers became so bad that this band of hard-working people had had enough – enough of suffering at the hands of ruthless mine owners and uncaring merchants such as Mr Cuthbert Alder, men who would slash prices and raise tolls to maximise their own profits. So, in desperation, they went on strike.

The general sentiment across the city was one of pity for the keelboat families but not from Cuddy Alder, who travelled to Parliament to ask that an Act be passed that would allow him to have the striking keelmen arrested and the strike broken. However, the Act was declined and so, in spite, Alder was known to parade his horse and coach along the picket line and throw through the window half-eaten chicken legs at the feet of the starving men.

Things went from bad to worse for the keelboat families. As the strike lengthened and winter approached, family members began to starve, and so eventually a closed meeting of key members of the boating community was held and a vote was taken on the idea of a number of night-time raids of the merchant food stores scattered across the city. The vote was unanimous and that very night the first raid took place.

However, the next morning, the sentiment of the city changed. Mr Cuthbert Alder took it upon himself to become the spokesman for the city's merchant class and to deepen the growing bad feeling that was spreading across the city towards the striking families. He organised a public rally, and to ensure a good attendance he ordered Mrs Brailsworth to make hundreds of goose pies and these he offered as good fare to anyone who would listen to his words. The rally was well attended and Alder twisted the knife, offering, once again, to take the road to London to appeal to Parliament.

That night, by lamplight, the keelmen met again but this time there was more than food on their minds. Alder had insulted them personally and the decision was taken to pay him a visit, and once they had finished with him, they might help lighten his larder a little.

The next evening under the cover of darkness, a small band of the hardest keelmen, armed with cudgels, set off across the city to Longbenton and the residence of Cuddy Alder, who was that very night entertaining a large group of travelling merchants. His table was straining under the weight of his hospitality.

The keelmen made their way onto the property as quietly as they could, unaware of the company of men within, and began to cross the courtyard towards Alder's door. But just then, a stableman emerged from the darkness and gave out a cry. Alarm spread quickly and Cuddy rallied his army of merchants with firearms and swords. They spilled out into the courtyard and set upon the keelmen, who, armed only with wooden clubs, suddenly found themselves hard pressed.

All would have gone from bad to worse for the keelmen if a very unlikely hero had not come to their aid. As Cuddy Alder barked orders to his men, suddenly an Amazonian-like cry rang out across the yard that stopped everyone in their tracks.

After years of biting her tongue and pent up anger towards Mr Alder and his like, Mrs Brailsworth let loose. However, she didn't stop there. Armed with her famous cleavers, she set about the merchants with a rage that none of the men had witnesses before. This gave fresh spirit to the keelmen and together they began to take the upper hand, beating Cuddy Alder and his merchant friends back behind their door.

As several stood guard, Mrs Brailsworth and the others helped themselves to the wealth of the larder and, before anyone knew it, they were away into the night with all of Cuddy Alder's goose pies.

Later that night, there was a great feast upon the floating village of the keelboat families, and all ate their fill. Mrs Brailsworth sat among them as

Goose Pie

guest of honour, for she had never forgotten her roots and knew that she was with her own.

Well, I would like to say that the story ends well, but unfortunately it's not quite that kind of tale. Cuthbert Alder had all the ammunition he needed and so, a few days later, he travelled south to London and was able to secure the Act that he so desperately desired. You see, rich men stick together, too. When he returned north, the ringleaders of that daring raid were arrested and, as an example to the rest of the keelboat families, they were taken to the town moor and became the first people in thirty years to be hanged there.

About Living on Boats

There are a number of repetitive questions that come up from non-boat-dwellers about life on a narrowboat: 'Can you stand up straight?'; 'Is it cold in winter?'; 'Have you got a toilet?' and 'Where do you live when you're not on the boat?'

In reality, life on board is very comfortable. You can change your neighbours any time you like and, yes, we have a toilet. I wouldn't choose to live on land again.

In the past, however, it was a very different story. The notion of families living on boats was late on in the history of the canals, and for the large part, working a boat was very much like any other job, boat workers would go home at the end of work, just like anybody else. It was only later, when the incomes of boatmen were squeezed, that, due to necessity, whole families moved on board.

You have to remember that on our boat, we have the whole 70ft boat length to carve up into living space, but back then families moved in to the boatman's cabin, because the majority of the boat was needed for haulage. To be fair, however, compared to other working-class dwellings at the time, living conditions on board were good, apart from being cramped. Families with older children often took on a butty boat, which was towed behind. It gave the family the ability to carry extra loads and provided a second living space.

The main issue was social separation. A whole culture developed and, due to its transient nature, became isolated from settled communities, which, in turn, led to ill feeling and suspicion until eventually boating families kept themselves to themselves. They taught their own children away from mainstream schools, where boat children were badly bullied, and stopped accessing other facilities including healthcare.

All this eventually led to interest from the churches and the setting up of boaters' missionaries, but it's hard to tell how well attended these were. There was a woman called Sister Mary Ward, who lived in Stoke Bruerne. She made a connection with the boating community and because they grew to trust her, they started to visit her for medical attention. She wasn't qualified but undertook the procedures that nurses would have carried out and provided medicines from her own pocket. She said, 'You can't take me away from the boat people. There isn't one of them wouldn't die for me, or one I wouldn't die for.'

CHRISTMAS ON THE CUT

In the December of 1836, winter hit very hard and it hit very quickly, and in Wolverhampton Wharf, a place where large numbers of boats would gather for offloading and reloading before carrying out journeys across the country, the canal froze overnight. The ice became so thick that even the ice-breaking boats had to give up for fear of damage to their hulls. The canal was on lockdown.

In the wharf stood the toll house, marked out by its large bay window and hexagonal structure designed to allow the toll officer, a man named Darcy, a full view of the yard. The previous day, before the deep freeze, Darcy had gauged the weight of all the loaded boats and had provided each boat owner with a chit with their individual toll charge written on it.

Now, Darcy was a young man with a lot to prove and he wore his superiority like a badge. He could be seen daily, striding around the wharf, the toll house keys swinging from his belt to remind people of his status and, if that wasn't enough, on the other side of his belt he carried a blunderbuss, just in case anyone considered trying to leave without paying – and payment was due in the morning.

That morning, most of the boats in the wharf were due to leave – not before, of course, settling their debt with Darcy. However, with the freeze and the ice nothing could move. In fact, as the boat families assessed the situation, they came to the conclusion that this was going to be a long wait indeed and if they couldn't move then they couldn't earn, and if they couldn't earn then they couldn't eat, and things were likely to turn desperate fairly quickly.

So, their only option was to plead to the good nature of Darcy. If he would allow them to hold on to the toll money they owed, on the premise that it would be repaid in the future, then the families might just scrape by. What they didn't appreciate was that Darcy didn't have a good nature. He listened to the plight of the boatmen with a look of amusement on his face and then, as he casually patted the blunderbuss at his belt, he refused to help and demanded that he receive the toll.

After receiving the money, Darcy took it to the toll house and placed it into the safe where it would stay with the other monies collected over the last month. It was nearly Christmas and so the wharf owners, Darcy's bosses, had arranged to visit to take possession of the profits in the New Year.

Meanwhile, in the yard there was a gathering. Men and women off the boats came together to try to find ways of supporting each other through what was going to be a pretty difficult time. With next to no money, very little provisions and children to feed, they were desperate. Eventually, as the conversation continued everyone agreed that there was only one person who could help.

There was, at this time, a local health inspector, a man by the name of Joseph Conway. His job was to take an interest in the welfare of boating families. He knew that, contrary to the rules outlined by the haulage companies, whole families were aboard these boats and he made a point to try and help where he could.

The boating families were very close knit and outside help was very rarely accepted, but Conway was a decent man and had earned the trust of the boaters. He made sure, as much as he could, that healthcare was available; the births of the children were overseen by experienced midwives; and the boat children were taught lessons and religion.

It was because of this trust that a small group of boatmen went to visit Conway and explained the situation. After listening carefully to all that the men had to say, Conway agreed to help.

Christmas Eve came and Mr Darcy was a busy man. His job today was to shut down the wharf and ensure that everything was safely locked away and the tollhouse was clean and ready for his New Year visit from his bosses. And, of course, it was Christmas and so he had every intention of taking a well-earned day of rest.

During these preparations Conway arrived, and the two men spoke for some time. Conway gave a good case for the boat families. He described in detail the conditions that they were facing and requested that Darcy look into his heart and, if nothing else, feel the spirit of the season and show some charity. But, of course, true to his nature, Darcy allowed Joseph to finish talking, showed him a sly smile and then told him, with just a little bit too much enjoyment in his voice, what he could do with his charity. He left Conway in the yard as he went to finish locking down the tollhouse and set off to enjoy his Christmas at the house the canal company provided as part of the job.

Conway took the time to relay the bad news to the boating families and it broke his heart to see the look of despair in their faces. He didn't know what to do or say that would in any way make the situation any easier, and so in desperation he clutched a thought and said that they shouldn't give up hope and that Christmas was a time for miracles. His words didn't help and the boaters turned their backs as well.

Later that evening, as the temperature dropped even lower, Darcy finally made his way home. He took one last look at the toll house to make sure that all was secure and then, without a backwards glance towards the suffering families, he left. As he made his way through the cold Wolverhampton streets, his heavy overcoat pulled tight around him, he glimpsed the lights of a local inn and decided to make a stop to warm himself before making for home.

The inn was warm and cosy, and Darcy knew the ale was good, so he bought himself a drink and found himself a corner table, removed his keys and blunderbuss, placed them on the table and settled down to enjoy a glass in his own company. Well, I'm sure that you know as well as I do that one rarely stays as one, and after a few hours Darcy had warmed himself well, having drunk more than his fair share of ale.

He was just starting to stand and make his unsteady way home when who should come through the door but Joseph Conway. Conway took one look and turned to leave but Darcy was quick and loudly asked him where he was going. Did he not like the company of his betters? Did he prefer the company of boatmen, people with minds as thick as the silt at the water's bottom?

Conway's fists clenched as he turned and, before anyone could stop them, the two men began to fight. Conway threw himself at Darcy, taking the two of them and the table on to the floor. The brawl continued for a few minutes before they were separated by the landlord and Darcy was ordered to leave. Conway stayed on to clear up and explain the situation.

The next morning was Christmas, and as the sun rose, boating families all around the basin awoke in their frozen cabins to stoke fires and enjoy as meagre a Christmas as they could remember. Smoke began to rise in the air and as there was no wind, the smoke from the boats' stovepipes rose in straight lines. The scene could have been idyllic had it not been for the situation on board the boats.

One old boatman climbed out from under his blankets and quietly, so as not to disturb his sleeping family, made his way to the cabin hatch so that he could step out and greet the day. However, as he unlocked and stepped out onto the back deck, he found a box blocking the way that hadn't been there the night before. Well, he scratched his head and bent to open it, only to find, to his surprise and amazement, that the box was filled with food, a few bottles of ale and wrapped gifts. He couldn't believe it and, as he picked up the box, he noticed that he wasn't alone. On the back deck of every boat in the wharf, boxes had been left by who knew who. Well, excitement quickly spread, as did the Christmas spirit, and before anyone knew it, the wharf was bustling with life.

Meanwhile, in the city, Darcy woke that morning to a bad head. He climbed out of bed with a groan and tried to make sense of the evening before. As he recalled how he had got a rise out of Conway he smiled, and it took a little of the sting out of his aching head. And so to enjoy the day, he thought to himself.

He crossed his room to the tangle of clothes that he had drunkenly dropped the night before and began to dress, but as he did, he immediately knew something was wrong. His belt was somewhat lighter than it should be, and he realised that his keys were missing. Fear rose in Darcy's mind as he desperately tried to remember his actions the night before, when suddenly he remembered that he had taken his keys from his belt and left them on the taproom table.

Hurriedly, he left his house and ran to the inn, hoping for all his worth that his keys had not been taken. When he arrived, the innkeeper made him sweat by berating him at length for fighting on his premises but eventually, to Darcy's relief, the innkeeper produced his keys and blunderbuss and told him to be on his way. As Darcy put the items back on his belt, he felt whole again, but as he walked out on that cold Christmas morning a little niggle started in the back of his mind and slowly he made his way down to the tollhouse, just to make sure all was well.

The sight that met him was one that he would never really recover from. Against all odds, Christmas had come to Wolverhampton Wharf. Boatmen and women laughed and sang around fire-filled braziers, children played and danced. Darcy stood with his mouth open in horror as a thought took shape in his mind.

Slowly, he came back to life and moved swiftly to the tollhouse door. With a shaking hand, he put the key to the lock and turned. he entered the room and at first all looked as it should be – but then he saw it, the door to the tollhouse safe was open, its contents gone.

Anger slowly spread through Darcy's body and he stumbled out of the house and into the yard. Anger turned to sickness as he approached the boats and saw men raising bottles in cheer. He shouted above the noise, demanding to know who had stolen the money, and threatening them with the power of the law. The boat people stood in silence until one of them spoke for the rest – and he spoke the truth when he said that none of them knew what had happened. All they knew was that Father Christmas must be real indeed, and they laughed long and hard.

Darcy lowered his head and turned to leave when he saw Conway coming down to the wharf. Suddenly his anger returned, and he confronted him, demanding that he find the thief and return every penny that had been taken. Joseph Conway listened to every word that Darcy said and then quietly, and with a well-deserved smile on his face, pointed out that maybe he should stop thinking about finding thieves and start thinking about excuses, especially as to why his keys had been missing for a whole evening while they should have been safe upon his belt. Once again, Darcy fell silent. All the colour drained from his face and he stared into space. The boaters watched him walk like a man condemned from the wharf – and most of them never saw him again. But, as for Joseph Conway? He spent the day with his friends and many more besides, and that's about as much as I know about this little Christmas tale.

About the Boatman's Cabin

Boatmen's cabins are amazing spaces. Look inside and they draw you in. Investigate further and you realise just how clever they are. A cupboard that looks like a cupboard folds down to become a bed. Close that, and open another, and you can all sit down for your tea because it's not a cupboard, it's the table. The seats you're sat on are your storage. And on it goes, and all the time there's the stove in the corner keeping the place as warm as toast. Every available bit of space is used, but it's not just practical it's also full of style. It has to be – this isn't just a working space, it's a home.

In those working days, you were judged by the brightness of your brass. It wasn't just the inside that counted, though. The early working boats weren't decorated to start with but eventually the style known as 'Roses and Castles' started to appear and pretty soon every possible part would be painted. No one really knows where the panels of castles and floral really came from, but the brushstroke petals were quick to paint and soon even horses' harnesses had roses on them. As women joined men on working boats, crochet also took off, with lace decoration wherever it would fit, as trimmings on woodwork and even as horses' ear caps.

I like this story, it says a lot about living in small spaces.

A Boater's Affair

There was once this man who was a bit of a rogue and a charmer of people. Well, to get by in the world, he had found that it was easier to persuade others that their money and possessions would be better placed with him than kept to themselves, if you know what I mean, and he was very good at it, or so the story says.

Well he had chanced his luck with all manner of people – merchants' wives and old ladies of wealth – but he had never considered trying to gain the confidence of a boat owner's wife before, had never thought that working folk were worth the effort. Until one evening, he overheard a conversation between a man and a woman who ran a narrowboat up and down the cut, taking all manner of goods to all manner of places, and when he heard of the kind of things that were on board an idea came to the mind of that wicked wit.

You see, this husband and wife, they owned a working boat, back in the day when working boats were working. They had so much to do, what with hauling goods and fending for their four children, who also lived on board, that they found themselves in need of help. And so, they put the word out that they were after a 'chap', as men who helped out on boats used to be called, to come live and work alongside them – good rates of pay and board would be provided.

Well, the fella planned it to the letter, so he did. Waiting for the husband to be out and about, he politely knocked on the boat and as the wife came to the cabin door, all flustered for looking after the kids, he didn't half flash her a nice smile and it was well rehearsed and often used and she fell right for it.

Now, don't get me wrong because I'm not blaming her at all, the husband he fell for it too. By the time he came home, the charmer had wormed his way on board, had been fed and watered and now had the kids sat quiet as mice listening to one of his various tall tales. The husband couldn't believe his ears nor his eyes and when the story was done, he set about employing the man.

All went well, or so it seemed. What the rogue lacked in experience, he made up in enthusiasm, and pretty soon he was doing as well as any old boater. But what the couple didn't know was that, at night time, because the man slept among the cargo he had free rein to help himself. Well, he wasn't foolish, this fella, and he knew to only help himself to bits. For example, he might drain off one or two bottles of brandy to sell on the sly, but to make sure that the barrel wasn't light he would top the thing up with canal water so no one would notice. A little here and a little there made him a shilling or two but this wasn't the real prize, nor the bigger picture – oh no, it was only the start.

All the time he worked on that boat he was actually working at driving a wedge between husband and wife, for he had a mind to take over the boat. He would throw her that smile and she would smile back, and she started over time to compare the two men in her life. The wit, he was handsome and charming and clean, whereas her husband was gnarled with hard work and grunted most of the time. The rogue, he was gentle around the children, gave them time and lavished them with stories of high adventure, where her husband was harsh and could talk of nothing but the cut, for it was all he had ever known. The charmer would bring her small gifts, nothing fancy and not often enough to cause offence – sometimes it was nothing more than a flower from the towpath – but it all helped to make sure that over time he could do no wrong and the husband was more than likely in the dog house. This fellow now had his feet fully under the table.

The rogue's intention was to work the situation up to such a frenzy that she would push the husband out, and the husband himself would feel so dark about being there that, once pushed, he would be glad to leave. He talked to the husband all the time, as they worked, about the world away from the towpath; the easy life, the life of a roving man with nothing to tie you down. The more he painted that picture, and the worse things got between husband and wife, the more appealing that lifestyle seemed.

Do you know what? He just about got away with it and was days away from making his move, but the story tells that he made a simple mistake. It was nothing really, but it did send the whole thing off in the other direction. You see, as they moored up one good autumn day and busied themselves with jobs about the boat, the children went off playing in the fields, not too far away, for they knew not to go too far. They found some apples dropped from an old apple tree. Well, the young ones gathered them up and made to take them back to their mother, but the rogue, he got in the way and told the children that they owed him the apples for all the stories he had told. He only half-meant it really, but as they refused, he got angry. He felt that he already owned the boat himself and so he took the apples and the children ran away.

I'm sure that he felt he could do what he liked and that he had charmed the wife so much that she would clip the children's lugs for telling tales – and the husband wouldn't care either – but when she found out she saw red. You see, the man had never met boaters before. He didn't understand that living like they did caused a bond that a wedge just couldn't split and when she heard what he had done she went looking for him.

She gave him a piece of her mind – and it was a really big bit of her mind because it went on for some time. In fact, she was so drained by the end of her monologue that she had to drink ale to cool herself down. Well, the charm stopped there and out came his temper. He thought to himself that if he didn't tame her now, he never would and would never have the boat. So he too drew some ale, and he took a bit of his mind and threw it right back at the wife.

The row continued for some time and didn't just stay at the boat. Goodness knows where the husband had been during it, the story doesn't tell, but when he got to the boat the chap and the wife had drunk all the ale and had taken the argument off to the inn up the road. When the husband walked in through the door, the sight that met him shocked him. I'm sure. The two grown-ups were nose to nose and the children were bleating like lambs. Enough was enough.

'She is still my wife!' thought the man, and he stood in the way of chap and told him, in no uncertain terms, that he would not have his wife spoken to like that and he would happily take him outside if he wanted to take the issue any further. And you know, as he said it and in the way that he did, it was like a spell was broken for the wife and she saw her husband anew. She saw him as the man she had married all of them seasons ago.

This rogue, this charmer, he could sense he was on the ropes. But he did have one last peg to drive between them, and as the husband stood there all red of face, very calmly and quietly didn't he lean forward and tell the husband what the wife and himself had been up to any time they had the chance and the husband's back was turned.

It was like time stood still for the husband, and all the colour drained from his face as he turned to face his wife and ask her if this was true. She looked at him, her husband, and all the anger dropped from her face and she said to him, simple like, 'If you have to ask, then you surely don't love me at all.' She turned to leave, but just before she walked out of the door, he spoke.

'Wife,' he said. 'I always loved you and always will, just lost sight of it somewhere I did. It's this wicked man that's the liar and I know that it's true, and I also know what we both have to do.'

And with that, husband and wife, they beat that rogue black and blue and drove him so far away from the cut that he never ventured near a boat, nor a married couple again.

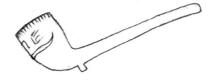

ABOUT THE LOCKS

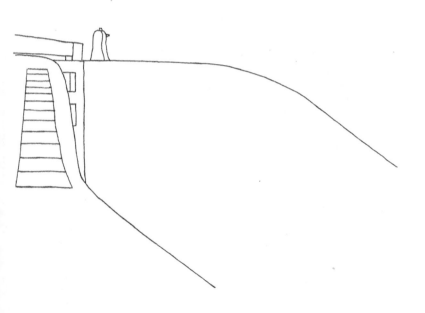

There's this thing that you can do, if you want to, and I don't want you, in any way, to think that I am advocating bad behaviour. Far be it from me, but you can do this if you want to. It's best saved for someone that's rubbed you up the wrong way. Narrowboats are small spaces at times and it's not always possible to not fall out, and so if a certain person has really got your goat, this is what you do.

You ask them, in a really nice way, if they would like to learn how to work a lock, and then you take them, ahead of the boat, up to the lock mechanism. Now, they don't always have them, so you will have to pick your time right, but on the ground, you should see a grate cover with lots of little holes in it. Now, this is the tricky bit. You have to manoeuvre your 'friend' so that they are standing right over the grate, but do it in a way that they don't get suspicious, and then put your windlass onto the mechanism and get your 'friend' to open the lock.

What should happen at this point is that the water being forced by gravity through the gate and into the lock will travel at such a rate that some of it will be directed at a fair pace up through the grate with a right big gush and your 'friend' will have to go back to the boat and change their pants. Revenge is yours!

We have the Chinese to thank for locks. They were using them a very long time ago but essentially, they are there to get boats up and down hills – and they do it pretty well. Me and Jo have a love–hate relationship with them. When you have all the time in the world they are great, especially on those hot summer days when people are out and you get a crowd watching, but a lock won't be rushed. It just causes accidents, rushing around locks, and on cold, wet days when you just need to get to where you are going, the thought of locks can really make you wonder why.

I will tell you something for nothing though: getting to the end of a day when you have just done a big flight, there's no better feeling.

THE LOCK RACE

In the pub one night two old boaters, man and wife as it happens, were having a quiet pint at the end of the bar when they found themselves getting into a conversation with a local railwayman. This fella, he was passionate about the trains and started going on about how they're the only way forward and speed is the key. He boasted about how, pretty soon, if the railway expanded in the way that was planned, they'd be able to get anywhere in the country at the drop of a hat – and in style.

Well, the wife could see her husband's knuckles going white and so she tried to steer the conversation on to other matters, but the railwayman was having none of it. He really had started to enjoy himself and the effect it was having on the husband. He started to describe the future and he made it very clear that his vision of the future did not include boats, 'because', he said, 'there's no future in boats, they are just too slow'.

Well, the comment was like a red rag to a bull and the husband pushed back his stool and made to confront the railwayman. Luckily for everyone, the landlord was quicker. He got out from behind the bar and stood firmly between the two to try to play the diplomat. 'That's enough!' said the landlord. 'If you can't find a way to settle this, then you can take it outside. I'm having no trouble in here.'

The two men stared at each other for a few seconds, and the landlord feared the worst, when suddenly the railwayman spoke up, 'How about a wager?' Well, that got the attention of the rest of the people in the bar, ears pricked up at the mention of a bet. 'There's a load of timber wants taking down to Frodsham. It's bound for Birkenhead and will need to be loaded onto trucks by 8.30 p.m. on Friday. If you can get it there ready for loading, then you win the bet.'

'But tomorrow's Wednesday,' pointed out the wife.

'Well, you'd better get a shift on then,' replied the railwayman, and he and the husband both spat on their palms and shook hands.

The next morning, it was early as the boat was loaded with the timber and the husband and wife were stood close together, discussing whether it was, in any way, possible to make this journey in time. With the number of locks along the route, it would only take a bottleneck of boats in the way or the locks to be set against them to slow them down and the bet would be lost, but the husband had shaken hands so they would just have to try. Not too soon after, they received a nod to say that all the goods were safe on board and they could get underway, and with a chorus of 'Good luck!' from the loading team, they untied and set off.

They had twenty-one locks to navigate before they got to Wolverhampton and then eventually onto the Shropshire Union Canal. However, the husband and wife team were well rehearsed, each knowing their role, and they made good progress. But it just seemed that every lock was set against them and it slowed them down. They could sense the time slipping away but they pushed on and – would you know it – as they reached the twelfth lock, its gates were already open and the boat could move quickly inside. Well, they were in and out in no time and off to the next, which again, to their surprise, was open. They looked all around to see if anyone was messing with the gates but there was no one to be seen so the only explanation was that Lady Luck was finally shining and by 10.30 that evening they pulled the boat in at Norbury, 32 miles from where they had started.

They lay in their bed that night in near silence. Neither of them was young, and the day had taken its toll on their bodies and, with being so focused on the task, their minds as well. With another two long days ahead, each was worried about the other – but these were working folk, and they had each other. There, in the darkness of the cabin and under the warmth of their blankets, hand slipped into hand and the wife heard her husband say, simply, 'Thank you'.

They were both up and off by 3.30 the next morning – Drayton locks were 10 miles away and they were keen to get going and they managed it before daybreak. After a quick brew, they took a deep breath and set off down the five locks, followed quickly by another five at Adderley and fifteen hard locks at Audlem. However, it was halfway down these that they started to realise, once again, that the locks were all in their favour. But not just that, as they ploughed along, other boats seemed to hold back and let them have the conveniently open gates; often there would be another boater around who just happened to be on hand to help get them through; and by the time they reached the two locks at Hack Green, a

small crowd had gathered to help, which meant that the
pair didn't even need to get off the boat.

With the headway that this gave them, they passed
Nantwich in good time and were feeling good in themselves. As they passed the end of the Llangollen Canal,
they exchanged a look and began to believe that this was
possible after all. On to the Middlewich branch they
went, and down four more locks before they entered the
Trent & Mersey Canal, down a flight of three through
the famous Big Lock – aptly named because it is a very
big lock – and finally they arrived at the Anderson
Boatlift by nightfall.

That night, the husband and wife decided to reward
themselves. Whatever happened tomorrow, they had
worked two long days, and supper in a local pub was in
order. Besides, the husband wanted to ring through to the
railwayman just to make sure that everything was in order
for the offload.

'You'd best have them trucks ready for when we get there,' the husband said.

But when he told the railwayman where they had got to, he laughed, and said, 'Even if you had sails, you will never make it in time!'

The couple ate their food in silence. The telephone conversation had left them feeling flat and neither wanted to talk about the next day's journey. Eventually they decided to leave. However, when they went to pay their bill, the landlord told them, 'It's paid for, it's on the house. I've heard of your journey, we all have, and we wish you all the luck in the world!'

Well, that bucked them right up and they walked back to the boat with smiles on their faces.

It was a loud knocking that woke them early the next morning, and as they opened the back hatch, blinking in the light, they saw the face of a heavy-set man staring in at them. 'We don't start till 8, as a rule, but we've heard what you're doing. We've heard about your bet, it's gone 6 and the lift's ready if you are?'

The boatlift seemed to take forever, but it didn't really, husband and wife were just keen to be off. As the boat moved away, the heavy-set man shouted loud enough to hear over the noise of the engine, 'Don't worry, they're ready for you at the Saltersford lock!'

They went flat out, the winding miles disappearing behind them, as was the time, but suddenly they heard a shout and as they looked up ahead they could see the lockkeepers waving them in. 'On to Dutton,' one of them said. 'Sound your horn as you meet the corner and the boys there will have it open.' They shook hands with the two of them and, with a shout of thanks, were off again.

They were in and out at Dutton with hardly a word, and as they left, they realised they only had the Frodsham swing bridge and they had done it. They pushed on, hearts pounding, engine chugging hard, until eventually they saw it. The swing bridge was in sight. The wife stretched out a hand to sound the boat's klaxon but she needn't have bothered – the bridge was moving before she got the chance – and as they passed under, they received a sly wink from their new friend, the banksman.

And then they were there. They could hardly believe it, but they were there. The wife worked the tiller, bringing the boat over to the bank, and the husband threw a line to the towpath and the banksmen pulled them in. Husband and wife stood shoulder to shoulder, watching the timber being craned onto the waiting trucks, and as the last load was being shifted, they were aware of a familiar face. Standing near the loaded trucks was the railwayman with a very unhappy look on his face and his pocket watch in his hand.

Husband and wife had forgotten all about the time. They were just happy that they had made the journey and were still taking in how much their cause had been shared by others who were as passionate about boats as themselves. The husband pulled his watch from his waistcoat pocket and opened its cover to see the time – 8.30 p.m. on the nose.

'Who says boats are slow?' he said, loud enough for everyone to hear, and then walked over to receive their well-earned reward from a less-than-boastful railwayman.

About a Boatman

This next story came from our mate, Pete Boyce. We first met Pete up in Whitby at the big folk gathering and once you've met his great big smile, you can't forget it. Pete is the owner of the historic working boat, *Renfrew*, a big Northwich from the Grand Union Canal Carrying Company, and what's really wonderful is that Pete and *Renfrew* are still carrying. They transport timber for narrowboat carpentry and restoration.

The Ghosts in the Cutting

On many canals there are deep cuttings and sometimes, if you look closely enough, you can work out that these deep cuttings used to be tunnels. The tunnels were eventually opened out to improve traffic flow and speed. However, in one such tunnel there was a dog-leg halfway through, where the tunnellers digging into the hill from each end did not quite meet head on – well, this left a kink, and also a ledge, halfway through, which can still be seen to this day.

So, back before the tunnel was opened up, there just happened to be this young boatman who was starting to consider marriage, but he had a bit of a problem. He really wanted to marry a girl from his own people – a girl from a good boat family. However, everyone was busy on their moving boats, carrying goods for the canal company and industries along the cut, so there was just no chance of spending any time with any girl if you fancied them, unless by some miracle you both ended up at the same stoppage for maintenance or you were loading in the same yard, or at the same pub in the middle of your trip. Even then, it was a case of, 'how do?' as you met and the horse line was passed over the cabin; a 'Fine thanks!' as the boats moved off in opposite directions; and a shouted, 'See you next week!' as you went round the bend. It was just very rare that you were travelling in the same direction at the same time.

However, as luck would have it, the young boatman found time enough one trip to ask this girl to marry him, and she, to his amazement, said, 'Yes'. Well, he had his younger brother working with him at the time and had to ask him to leave the boat, so that once they were married, she could come aboard to be with him all the time. And that, dear friends, is when the problems started.

Living together all the time showed up their little habits and weaknesses – and most definitely their differences. Well, you see, his big problem was his laziness around the boat, which he didn't see as a problem as he made money. Her problem was that she was a nag, and he was hounded by her, morning, noon and night.

Eventually, the young boatman had had enough, and he thought of a solution to his problem. By all accounts, he devised a very drastic way of putting an end to her nagging. He waited until the next time they were in the tunnel, the horse was being led over the top of the hill, and he was lying on the bows of the boat, legging off the tunnel walls to get the boat through. He waited, because he knew it was coming, until she started on at him from the hatches in the stern, and that's when he acted. He jumped up and ran back along the top plank when they were halfway through and shouted, 'Stop your nagging or I'll put you on the ledge!'

Her reply was instant. 'No you won't!' she shouted. 'Now, get back to your legging!'

Well, that was it, and as quick as a flash, he shot into the boat, grabbed his wife and dragged her outside, threw her down on to the ledge and shouted, 'When you stop your nagging, I'll come and fetch you!'

Of course, in his mind it was only a joke and he had every intention of stopping the boat and coming back for her, when suddenly he heard a splash. In a panic, he tried desperately to stop, but it takes a while to stop 25 tons of loaded boat, and by the time he got back to his wife she was floating lifeless in the water.

'Drowned,' he related later to the police. 'She drowned and there was nothing I could do.' Well, the lad had never been in trouble in his entire life and so, being of good character, he was bailed, awaiting the coroner. The double tragedy was that he was so haunted by what had happened that he took himself off to the pub at the locks and got roaring drunk. On his way back to the boat that he had shared for such a little time with his wife, he fell off the lock gate he was crossing and was drowned himself.

To this day, it's said that the couple haunt the tunnel, and when the wind blows on a stormy night, you can hear her nagging, and him forever wailing at the loss of his wife.

Pete says that this was told by an old boatman to the BBC in the 1960s, and when asked if he believed the story, he said, 'No, I don't believe in ghosts, and I've never heard them. I'm always sure I'm in the cabin for that stretch.'

ABOUT THE DECLINE

Nothing lasts forever, as they say – or does it? The canal system that fed the biggest industrial shift in our history actually lasted until the 1960s, but in the end just couldn't compete with the road and rail improvements that had taken place and, in particular, the shift from coal gas to North Sea gas.

However, this isn't to say that the canals just closed and all became unused overnight. Some of the better-funded canals, like the Shropshire Union, continued to be used, but it was due to a new wave of enthusiasm that led to the canals being utilised in a very different way indeed.

Sadly, however, a lot of canals did go into disuse. Many of them were drained, some were filled in, and as for boating families? Well, most moved off the canals, never to return. In fact, boat children were told not to mention their heritage for fear that it might stop them moving into new trades. It was seen to some to be something shameful, although not to all.

Our inland waterways have moved on again. Back in the 1940s, the Inland Waterways Association was established to try and breath life back into the canals, but they were fighting an uphill battle against the government and British Waterways, who really just wanted them filled in. However, over time, they and an army of volunteers started to win the war. They got their hands dirty, digging out the old system, and so dawned the age of the pleasure boater.

But let's not forget the past as I think this last little story, quite pertinently, illustrates …

BLISWORTH TUNNEL

During the summer of 1973, a man hired a day boat for a short daytrip on the canal. His plan was to travel the short distance along the Grand Union from Stoke Bruerne, through Northamptonshire's Blisworth Tunnel, and end his journey at the village of Blisworth itself.

The weather was blisteringly hot and so when he eventually entered the tunnel, the dark and coldness must have been a welcome escape from the heat and light. Well, the boat was underground for some time, but when the man finally brought the boat back out of the tunnel at the Blisworth end, it was clear that he had been changed by the experience. He wasn't frightened but it was obvious that he had seen something underground that would never leave him.

At midday, he pulled his boat in outside a canal-side pub and moored up before going inside to order some food, but as he sat at the bar his food sat untouched and he looked off into space, deep in thought. Well, it didn't go unnoticed and eventually, after a few nudges, the landlord approached the man and asked him if there was anything wrong with the food – did he want to order anything else? The man shook his head like he was waking from a dream and then looked at the landlord with a haunted look on his face. Eventually he spoke.

'I've seen the strangest of things … coming through the tunnel. I've just seen the strangest of things. It's a journey I've wanted to do for years, what with doing most of the other tunnels. I'd go so far as to say I love them. I love the darkness and the smell and how timeless they feel, but never in my life and in any tunnel I've travelled have I seen anything like what I have just seen.'

The man took a moment and a deep breath, and the landlord could see that he was visibly shaking and he told the man to take his time. He took up the story again.

'My eyes were just getting used to the dark and I'd got the speed right on the throttle when I noticed that up ahead in the tunnel there was light. It was well off in the distance, and I thought it must be a boat coming towards me, what with the tunnel being wide enough, so I would have plenty of time to move out of the way. But as I travelled on, closer to what must have been the middle of tunnel, I could see it was no boat at all … It was a strange light, dim and flickering, sometimes there and sometimes not. I slowed down as I came closer and moved to the right hand side, just in case, you know, but what I saw … well, I really just can't explain.'

He took another breath. 'There was a branch tunnel where there really shouldn't have been one, and as I looked along it to where the light was coming from, I could see a number of men, huddled together and lit by candle light. I knew they were sad – I could see it etched on their faces, the grief, like men condemned and there was the sound, so sad … the sound of crying coming from their mouths.'

The man paused one last time and it seemed to the landlord that he might not speak again, but he did. 'I called out to them. I asked them could I help, but in my heart, I knew there would be no reply and so I passed them by, left them to their grief. And do you know, I could still see the light, it was still visible many metres further along … well, what do you make of that?'

There was silence for a while as the landlord took it all in, and then softly, he told the man this story:

'There are many ghosts imprisoned in Blisworth Tunnel. The old boatmen called them Boggarts. They are left there as memories of a tragic past, like scars to remind us of the harsh truth of working lives. Some nights, when the wind whistles through the trees up near the tunnel entrance, you can almost imagine that it's the mournful cries of the many that went in and never came back out.

'You know, there was a boat that went in there once. An old steamer called *Wasp* went in all stoked up with coal to get through as fast as it could, but as it travelled through it met a boat being legged the other way. All would have been well, but work was being done in there and no one told them that there was only room for one boat to pass and so they struck. Well, the smoke from the steamer choked the two leggers and they passed out and drowned in the water. The crew of *Wasp* pushed the engine to get her out, but by the time they came out another was dead – three men who would never see light again.

'But it's not them bogarts that you have met. No, yours is an older scar. That tunnel was built in 1793, by a gang of navvies who worked by candlelight alone. Three whole years they worked away at it, from both ends at the same time, but when they met in the middle it wasn't quite straight. There was a kink, which caused a weakness that brought the rock down all around them.

'They say that they were down there for days, the candles slowly dying, the air disappearing until they breathed their last. They eventually got to them, but it was too late. They brought them out and buried them in navvy graves – that's to say that there were no names to show who was who.

'Eventually they got the tunnel open, but the kink is still there, and you passed through it today. It's known as Buttermilk Hall these days, and I've a mind that you've just had a glimpse of the past. But that's all it is now, so you have nothing to fear from the past and it makes for a good story, albeit a tragic one, and you are not the first to tell it. But that's what you should do, you should tell it so that none of us forget the men who really made the cut.'

After listening to the story, the man thanked the landlord and went on his way. The tale doesn't tell what happened to him after that. Maybe he left the boat where it was and found another way home, or it's possible he carried on to Blisworth and then went back to his life, but what I can tell you is that he did indeed pass on the story – he must have done, because now I have it and I've passed it on to you.

ABOUT THE END

Well, that's it. Our journey, for now, has to come to a stop, but it's not the end. Think of it as a bit like mooring up for the night. You can rest easy in your bed knowing that there are more adventures to come. We have a rich heritage in this country, one that needs to be celebrated, not just through the deeds of rich and privileged men. We need to spend a bit more time with our own folk, sharing their stories of good times and folly, because it's those stories that can teach us the most. Those stories are our stories to claim and make rich through the telling. The boatmen, women and children will never leave us. They are immortal, and their story cuts through the land like the eternal navigation, and while there's you and me around, there will always be someone to pass their story on.

Much love and light.

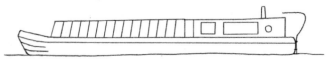

BIBLIOGRAPHY

Burton, A., *History's Most Dangerous Jobs: Navvies* (The History Press, 2012).

Chaplin, T., *The Narrowboat Book* (Whittet Books Ltd, 1978).

Corrie, E., *Tales from the Old Inland Waterways* (David & Charles, 1998).

Ellis, T., *The Sailing Barges of Maritime England* (Shepperton Swan, 1982).

Forster, E., *The Keelmen 1970* (Northern History Booklets, 1971).

Four Counties & the Welsh Canals (Collins Nicholson Water Guides, 2012).

Freer, W., *Canal Boat People 1840–1970* (PhD thesis, University of Nottingham, Nottingham ePrint, 1991).

Sadler-Moore, D., L. York & C.M. Jones, *Care on the Cut: 'Every Boater Matters', Sister Mary Ward BEM* (Del-Lor-Chris Publishing Co., 2015).

Unknown author, https://www.canaljunction.com/heritage.htm (accessed 16 January 2020).

Unknown author, https://www.waterwaysongs.info/
SongMenu.htm (accessed 21 January 2020).
Williamson, John, 'Interesting Reminiscences of
Ellesmere Port' (2017).

Society *for*
Storytelling

Since 1993, The Society for Storytelling has championed the ancient art of oral storytelling and its long and honourable history – not just as entertainment, but also in education, health, and inspiring and changing lives. Storytellers, enthusiasts and academics support and are supported by this registered charity to ensure the art is nurtured and developed throughout the UK.

Many activities of the Society are available to all, such as locating storytellers on the Society website, taking part in our annual National Storytelling Week at the start of every February, purchasing our quarterly magazine Storylines, or attending our Annual Gathering – a chance to revel in engaging performances, inspiring workshops, and the company of like-minded people.

You can also become a member of the Society to support the work we do. In return, you receive free access to Storylines, discounted tickets to the Annual Gathering and other storytelling events, the opportunity to join our mentorship scheme for new storytellers, and more. Among our great deals for members is a 30% discount off titles from The History Press.

For more information, including how to join, please visit

www.sfs.org.uk